# THE BRAVE HISTORIAN

ROBERT D. GAINES

Hidden Shelf Publishing House
P.O. Box 4168, McCall, ID 83638
www.hiddenshelfpublishinghouse.com

Artist: Megan Whitfield

Graphic design: Kristen Carrico

Interior layout: Kerstin Stokes

Gaines, Robert D.
The Brave Historian

ISBN: 978-0-9996466-8-7

Publisher's Cataloging-in-Publication Data

Names: Gaines, Robert D., author.
Title: The brave historian / Robert D. Gaines.
Description: McCall, ID: Hidden Shelf Publishing House, 2020.
Identifiers: LCCN: 2020909473 | ISBN: 978-1-7338193-6-7
(Hardcover) | 978- 0-9996466-8-7 (pbk.) | 978-0-9996466-7-0
(ebook)
Subjects: LCSH Centenarians--Fiction. | Authors--Fiction. |
Aging--Fiction. | Memory--Fiction. | Family--Fiction. |
Pennsylvania--Fiction. | BISAC FICTION / Literary | FICTION /
Absurdist
Classification: LCC PS3607 .A35955 B73 2020 | DDC 813.6--dc23

Printed in the United States of America

*Life is a lost and a wondrous rage,*
*I don't want to be afraid to be alone...*

# CHAPTER 1

It was stark, relentless.

John Hammond once again tried to shake the memory hammering inside his head. But, yes, there it was—strange men, without expression, ever so slowly lowering his little sister into the ground. Sweet, beautiful Sarah.

What had struck him as odd was that she didn't even move. Nothing, absolutely nothing.

It was miserable hot that day, bugs storming the yard as if this were some sort of picnic. And there was that fly again; that one particular fly darting from preacher to casket, then buzzing away, oblivious to its passage.

Mother was lost in black, father pale as a winter wind.

As flowers fell and dirt followed, John leaned close to his brother.

"I'm living to a hundred," he whispered bravely to David. "I'm never gonna die, never."

David said nothing, perhaps not even hearing. He too was lost.

That was the summer of 1910, nearly 90 years back. Peculiar, but beyond the stillness, John's most vivid memory was that one ugly fly, nasty brown with a streak of shimmering green, the kind you just want to squash. Yet, still to this day, its every detail remained permanently chiseled into his mind—a stupid fly.

And Sarah, at times John could barely remember what that little girl looked like, the sound of her voice, the feel of her fingers, the smell of her youth. She was just a vague and fleeting glance, like a startled dream seeking shelter from its awakened creator.

Such rotten luck, poor Sarah. She had only been three years old; now her big brother was nearing 100. Strange how she had fallen so quickly, and he had survived so long.

At the burial, father had vowed they would all meet again. John never bought it.

\* \* \* \*

In the twist of chance, John Garfield Hammond had arrived on earth barely one minute before midnight on December 31, 1899. His mother had kidded that hers would be the youngest child in Pennsylvania born in the old century.

Even as a child, John considered it a stroke of good fortune that he had not waited. His brush with the 19th century may have been brief, but nevertheless, he was there.

"You do know I have lived in two centuries," he would sometimes brag to his younger brother and sisters. Not long after Sarah's death, he realized that if indeed he managed to live 100 years, he also would be able to claim a third century on earth. To young Johnny Hammond, the concept of living to be a very old man carried a touch of excitement, an opportunity to calmly unwind and enjoy the easy life, good to be 100.

Now, as he neared the magical birthday, old John Hammond's frail body was a disaster of annoying pains and a punishing fatigue, his mind wandering recklessly through spheres of lost remembrance.

"Suck it up and carry your age with dignity," he would regularly demand within his mind, purposely pretending to be

6

somewhat of a pioneer poised to step into the 21st century. Once again, he was tired.

* * * *

In the dream, John was in the process of moving from Pennsylvania to California. Or was it the other way around? No matter, he still had not packed all his things, many of which were no longer even useful.

Looking through the old boxes inside an abandoned barn, John knew he would never be able to finish in time. He surely didn't need these things and should just take the easy course and toss everything. But inside one of the boxes he found a newspaper article from a baseball game he pitched in college. The headline was strikingly large and bold, "Hammond pitches Bucknell over Penn State." But, looking closer, John couldn't quite make out the date. And the newspaper looked almost new, as if printed by a computer. Did the date say 1999?

Is that possible? Did he still play baseball?

He paused to wonder if his arm was strong. He glanced at his grip and the seams of the ball, but his hands felt weak.

And now he noticed the date of the newspaper clipping had changed to May 2019. That couldn't be possible. That had to be at least 100 years wrong. He pulled out a book of charts and numbers, trying to figure if he still might be young. No, the date had to be a mistake.

A stream of noise disrupted his calculations; someone from outside the room yelling for him to hurry. Yes, he had almost forgotten he was packing to move. Quickly, he searched deeper into the box, tossing aside several crumpled items he could not identify, but then discovering a heavily bound book. Inside was a bunch of words that had mostly been crossed out and now had no meaning whatsoever. He decided to rearrange the sentences, perhaps to find perfection, but only became frustrated by this scrambled collection of unfinished thoughts. Again, that voice from somewhere outside beckoned for him to accelerate his work.

"There's too much," he shot back, throwing the different pages and notebooks to the ground.

Wait, what was this? He leaned closer to the scattered work as if uncovering a great mystery. Hidden inside the pages was a photograph of a beautiful woman; they most certainly had been deeply in love. He tried to remember, but the details seemed fuzzy and unreal. Wait, on the back of the photo was a scribbled and illegible name.

Who was she?

John tried to focus his thoughts, but now a group of strangers had broken through the barn door, demanding that he leave. They seemed to be furious, beyond reason.

"I just need to get all this together," he pleaded as they grabbed his arms and pulled him from his work. He tried to fight back, but the mob was too strong and he had no energy.

It was then that John grasped from somewhere within his sleeping brain that this was but a dream, thankful that he could not be harmed by the crazed intruders.

He felt his body relax, then wondered what else he might find in the boxes, but they were gone, the barn now empty. And he could feel his sleep dissolving, that it was 1999, although he was momentarily unsure where he lived . . . yes, California.

\* \* \* \*

John's eyes snapped open, his mind trying to capture the thoughts he was rapidly losing. Yes, he had been moving all his belongings. No problem, it was not real. John took a deep and cautious breath, thankful he no longer had to pack.

He just needed a few more minutes to rest, but his body would not move, and his mind would not stop as he suddenly fell into an awakened trance, now imagining himself wandering into the new century.

And what a spectacular plunge it would be. What with the nation gripped by millennium fever, his life story would be briskly hurled to center stage.

"John Hammond Enters Third Century of Life," would be the headline on the third page of the *New York Times*. No doubt *USA Today* would run the story front page above the crease.

He'd be on the cover of *Newsweek* and *People* and *Rolling Stone*. The late night celebrities would be relentless. *Good Morning America*, *60 Minutes* and *Entertainment Tonight* would rush their best anchors.

"And by the way," he would blurt to the press, "Now that I'm famous, I'd like to invite the top publishing houses to consider the many novels I have been carefully storing for this very moment in time."

No, that would be too brash, and some might think he was begging.

John chuckled to himself, applauding his brain's thirst for imaginary details, its ability to turn once intelligent thoughts into absurdity.

Why stop? Because once the word of his third century on earth began to spread, life would become crowded. Offers and contracts, commercials and TV movies, agents and lawyers, biographers and con artists, invitations to the White House and free vacations to the South Seas.

Certainly, John's dip into three centuries was not that unique. There were millions of centenarians in the world, but probably none had skimmed it so close.

By design, the interviews would be limited.

"You don't look 100 years old," grinning newscasters would say in unison. "What's your secret?"

"Well, I stay sharp with regular walks," John would reply, "and non-stop breathing."

No, John thought, they might confuse a clever quip with just being downright rude. It would be best to be thoughtful.

"My secret to living a long life," John would reply with a short pause to reflect serious consideration of the question. "I eat a lot of blueberries."

Yes, that would have them rushing to the grocery store.

Of course, with his birthday still a few weeks away, the media would be facing a possible problem. What if the old man should drop dead before then? Would they be forced to kill the story? No, the newscasters could just change the inflection of their voices.

"On a sad note," the anchor would stoically lament, "John Hammond died last night in his sleep, just a few days shy of accomplishing his goal to live in three different centuries.

"And now we go live to Fallbrook where Katy Bainbridge reports on an amazing array of treasures gathered by Ruby the Border Collie."

John stopped, tried to clear his mind, throw death in a garbage bag and toss it away. How absurd that an entire nation would be intrigued and concerned about a man who had been hounded by decades of lost opportunity and thickheaded failure.

John took another deep breath, scolded his untamed mind and returned to reality.

\* \* \* \*

THE BRAVE HISTORIAN

John understood that, like everything else, the celebration of the new millennium would come and it would go. He also knew there would be no more chances. Catch the ring and be a star, don't try and no one will ever know you even existed.

No, this time he would reach, he would grab, he would fight.

\* \* \* \*

A block from home, John entered the high school stadium. As always, his goal was once around the track, but today he was thinking perhaps a half mile, or maybe not. He moved slowly; bones creaking, mind clanking. Considering the human body is only designed for about 40 years of safe passage, he was a marvelous study of age. Sure, the skin was wrinkled and his hair had turned to thin white strands, but the internal signs were usually steady and, on the best of days, even strong.

John passed the 40-yard line, momentarily imagining he had the football and had just juked the last defender. Now at the 35, he was pulling away, heading for glory. About five minutes later, he had reached the goal line. "Touchdown Old John Hammond" the speakers blared within his head.

And a thought was triggered from another time, one he carefully tried to avoid, yet stuck to the floor of his brain like gravel.

There was another reason that might vault John and his three centuries into the national headlines. You see, here was the last of the legendary Hammond family. Enough said. Curiosity sparked. People would want to know more. There was another Hammond?

\* \* \* \*

In the first half of the 20th century, the Hammond family had sprinkled creative brilliance upon modern music, art, and literature. *The Three Hammonds*—John's father, brother and sister—were wild, sparkling, tumultuous. And hadn't they all died in rather bizarre circumstances?

George Hammond, John's father, was a whirlwind of music, composing hundreds of popular songs until his death in 1950. His music, mostly written from 1895-1910, was always characterized with a quick and raspy beat, horns that roared and drums that pounded. There was *Handlebar Boogie, Ticklin' My Horse* and *Sweet Suzie's Slippery Slide.* Hit tunes like *The Elephant Garden, Blue Skies of Mexico* and *Spittin' Up Wind* were played in every dance hall from New York to San Francisco.

A *Thump on the Rump* was one the most popular pieces of sheet music ever sold, until the summer of 1909 when George Hammond wrote *King of the Wild Animals.*

Although his music generally disregarded the rules of the day, the joy of its sounds could not be ignored.

"It's a crazed cyclone of never-ending noise," wrote one music critic. "The ears might throb, but the toes tap and the fingers pop. Mr. Hammond always stirs a gloriously fun headache."

George Hammond smiled, pushed, succeeded.

And then his music faded, almost vanished. It no longer had the vigor, the distinctive snap. Compositions turned stale, blasted by critics as "tired re-workings of past pleasures."

Many music historians would later say that the elder Hammond's early songs were the seeds for the music of the Roaring Twenties. But by then, in a musical era he was seemingly born to command, George could not revive his desire to create.

Perhaps he just took it inward. Perhaps he was no longer

hungry. Perhaps he no longer cared.

Interestingly, George Hammond had a brief resurgence late in his life. *Soft Return* was so different from any song he had ever written that it stunned the music crowd when it hit the market in early 1947, nearly four decades from the height of his popularity. The public, still in the mood to celebrate the end of World War II, somehow took it as a heroic victory tune. *Life Magazine* interpreted the song as "peace on a perfect spring morning."

But, really, it was nothing like that.

\* \* \* \*

In the spring of 1947, the *Saturday Evening Post* ran a story about the Hammond Family that included a photo of George with two of his adult children, David and Mary. John had known nothing about the article until seeing it on a colleague's desk at the newspaper office. He was stunned.

In this celebration of talent, Mary spoke about how George Hammond had always been her inspiration to create, and "the most wonderful father in the world." Even David grumbled a compliment about his childhood, quickly dismissing any sentiment and rambling into something about how his inner soul had no storage compartment and that one of the great insults of life was that you would forever be alone, and that family only mattered as a kick in the butt to get you out the door.

"He is so full of shit," John accidentally muttered out loud as he read the article. John's comment broke the silence of the workroom, several reporters looking up from their desks.

"Sorry," said John. "Just reading something. It's nothing."

John put his hands to his head as he continued to read. Of

course, he understood the anger and jealousy. It was the emptiness in his stomach that was most upsetting.

\* \* \* \*

In the photograph introducing the *Saturday Evening Post* article, George Hammond sat smiling at the piano, posed with his famous daughter and son.

Mary Hammond had become even more successful than her father, provided such terms could truly be measured. Both an oil painter and sculptor, she had long been considered one of the foremost artists of the 20th century. Her hands could twist the earth, grasp the soul. Her mixture of reality and imagination produced conscious-bending designs that are still skyrocketing in value.

As for John's brother, David was perhaps the darkest, the most volatile, and definitely the most difficult. There was nothing soft about him. The savage and unrelenting intensity of his many novels could tear holes through the senses, leaving the reader worn, demolished. To those who consumed his works, death would only heighten his fame.

These were *The Three Hammonds*, a gathering of magnificent eccentrics surely camping at the gates of insanity. Hell, they stormed the place. For in that mad dash for excellence, each was motored by a brain that simply would not slow down. Always thinking, always fighting, always plotting. To each of their minds, intellect was a blessing, a haunting.

The gears would clang, cells would ramble. Streams of thought piled recklessly into one another. No down time, no relaxation, no breaks.

It was a busy family, a famous family.

John, his mother Lillian and even George Hammond's later

wives had barely existed to the public. They were not news, so they really didn't matter.

Who was John Hammond? Just a sportswriter, a man bent on living forever.

* * * *

John was the oldest of the Hammond children. And, when it came to the two boys, he was clearly his father's favorite. David was quiet, anxious, a touch out of focus. Johnny was beautifully handsome, warm and energetic.

He shared his father's avocation for swapping stories over the evening fire. At times, he would retell father's old stories with new twists and meanings. Other times, his tales were conjured from his own blossoming mind. They were sensitive, awkward and often hilarious.

Even when John's stories fell a bit flat, the old man would hug his son.

"Let me rub that brilliant head of yours for good luck," George would tease. "You, Johnny, have got the talent."

Perhaps John did have the talent, but not the drive or the luck or that one key break that always seemed to be necessary for prominence.

It wasn't that John ignored fame. He wanted it desperately. He just never pushed hard for the chance at success. It's an old and worn out excuse, but it just never happened. He would have moments of supreme confidence, times of hard work and passionate gains. But it would always stop, always. Then, perhaps a week or a year or a moment hardly expected, his courage would be revived, only to ultimately crash again, forever engulfed in doubt.

It was the good times that were most inspiring, that he

wished he could somehow control.

John wrote music and stories, drew fascinating pencil sketches, wanted to be a baseball player, an actor, play the piano in an all-night bar. But he was stubborn, shy and never really followed through on anything that could provide an edge toward what he really wanted to do. He was always silently plagued by that subtle and childish fear of embarrassing failure. He didn't know where he picked it up, he just couldn't shake it.

Sure, he dreamed of being famous and surviving on his talents. It was just easier not to try, not to take a risk.

So John Hammond became a sportswriter at a daily newspaper. Hard-working and exceptional, but rather obscure considering the family credentials that he could have easily ridden to the heights of probably any career he might care to tackle. Instead, he wrote of other people's glories, silently envious he couldn't hit a baseball 400 feet or carry a football to daylight. Still, he was an outstanding writer, driven by a subtle passion that each word be significant.

> *By the fourth quarter, it was evident that the Michigan Wolverines were merely twisting through the wreckage of what had once been mighty Notre Dame.*

John was quite different than other sportswriters of the era. Most of his colleagues and adversaries seldom went beyond reporting who won the game and how they scored. They would pound out their features in less than an hour, then let their editors worry about such essentials as style and spelling.

Not John. He would strain to the brink of deadline, ever creating something different and powerful. Tightly shelved within the words of throwaway sports stories was a constant search for perfection.

> *Lou Gehrig had fallen quietly to Red Sox pitching this gray and misty afternoon at Yankee Stadium. Four disastrous attempts. Twice "strike three" was called, twice he swung through air. One dink foul into the stands back in the third inning was the only time his powerful club had touched a nail all day. Hardly a spark in this week-long Yankee plunge.*
>
> *Now sitting alone at his locker, Gehrig had an uncharacteristic growl to his voice.*
>
> *"It was only one game," snapped The Iron Horse in his best baseball lingo. "I've struck out before and I'll strike out again. I didn't do my part today, but tomorrow I'll be back. All that matters is that we lost. Tomorrow is another game. Tomorrow we just might bust this losing streak and win the next 15 straight. You just never know what will happen."*

John took pride in his unique and gifted talent for writing, even though he also realized his obsessive quest for perfection was essentially an anchor, forever holding him down.

He produced piles of wonderful features, but no fame.

Anyhow, what can you do with sports stories? You can write the finest account in newspaper history. Spend all night on one story. Go over the words again and again until you're certain nobody in the entire world could write a deeper or more meaningful portrayal of that ballgame. The readers will surely lose themselves in the finest 10 minutes of their entire day.

"Geez, your story was better than even being there," everyone will say. "Absolutely splendid. You should get a raise. You're too good for this paper. You ever thought about writing novels?"

Or maybe nobody will say anything at all, because all they really wanted to know was who won the game.

The thing about sports journalism, according to John, is that you also can write a piece of trash. Just pop out a lead, add a few quotes, don't forget to mention the score and go home. No problem.

"Nice story," someone might say.

Or, maybe not. Who cares? You've got to come back and write about another game the very next day anyway. You can be physically and mentally wasted from that masterpiece the day before, or you can be well-rested with plenty of time to look for better jobs on better papers and become drinking buddies with the guys who can get you there. It was soon clear to John that the happiest and wealthiest sportswriters couldn't write worth a shit.

John was a brilliant sportswriter—always working, always tired, always broke.

Someday, he figured, the big papers would call. They never did.

\* \* \* \*

Just because he wasn't famous, don't think John was the odd-ball of the family. No, he definitely had the Hammond bloodline. He carried the family gift as if it were a blessing from God.

You see, his mind never stopped working.

Always, the brain was a swirl of ideas, non-stop stories dancing long into the night on this most private stage, then heaved into a cloud of brilliance to be lost in the deepest pockets of his memory. For within John Hammond's infinite search for ingenuity, great thoughts seemed to continually escape to oblivion.

His excuse was well rehearsed, a victim of too many ideas to remember all of them. It definitely sounded like the perfect recipe for failure.

Still, some thoughts were captured into one of his notebooks. Or they were scratched haphazardly on pieces of paper and eventually tossed into cardboard boxes for future reference. Someday, he would put his ideas together. Someday, he would write a meaningful novel that would smash the world right between its polar caps.

Or perhaps his music would finally be heard.

For certain, he would never play professional baseball.

Inside a weary old man, John Hammond still searched for glory.

\* \* \* \*

John had been there, you know. He had once been strong, finally with a grip on contentment. It was not the first time for love, just the best.

Her name was Jessica Jones and they had met at Wrigley Field during the 1945 World Series in Chicago. She was a Cubs fan, but he loved her just the same.

She had innocence, desire. He was passionate, bold.

They talked the same level, the same tone. They listened, they joked, they argued about baseball. It was a fine and truthful understanding they shared.

She was 12 years younger than him, just turned 33. She was firm and tender and easily the most beautiful creature on earth. John burned in the pit of his stomach whenever he saw her or even thought of her. His mouth turned dry, his defenses scattered.

She claimed the same feelings. He was wise, handsome, virile. She was charmed by his maturity. And, really, he didn't look that old. God, she loved him with all of her heart. Or so it seemed for the longest time.

He brought her back to central Pennsylvania and they were married that same year, two days after Thanksgiving. They had a child two years later. It was September 3, 1947, a Wednesday, raining, the greatest day of his life.

They named her Sarah, after John's baby sister. Nothing could be so perfect. The child was quick and beautiful, even slept through the night.

And she was a delight to her Grandfather Hammond. The man once hailed as the "greatest living musical innovator on the planet" had not composed or written anything truly original since 1910. But in 1947 came *Soft Return.*

John, like many others, was floored by its incredibly beautiful and haunting sound. This was written by his father?

As far back as John could remember, George Hammond always seemed to be on the attack about one thing or another. And it was odd that a man who had once been so full of life could turn so bitter. But young Sarah made him proud, brought him back. She became everything to her grandfather.

He would visit nearly every day with a flower for Jessica and a kiss for Sarah. He would play with the child for hours, hold her gently on his lap, whisper funny stories and tickle under her chin.

"Let me rub that brilliant head of yours for good luck," George would tease his granddaughter. "You, my beautiful Sarah, have got the talent."

The little girl loved her grandfather.

And each time he played *Soft Return,* a dying George Hammond thought only of her.

# CHAPTER 2

The words had been hidden, locked in cardboard boxes stored deep in the attic. It was truly a lost treasure, these early writings. Brilliant ideas and scribbles scattered across a million pieces of paper.

And, yes, there it was, the first novel. Five years of work; pondering every word, carefully hiding every meaning. Truly, it was powerful, unique.

But, now, these were simply pages from a distant past.

Ever so slowly, John leafed through his ancient manuscript, his mind focused on an urgent search for significance. Some parts were electric, others rather stale. As always, he was uncertain as to value. Perhaps readers would find it vague or simply too bizarre. Then again, maybe he was just too critical, too much the perfectionist.

John had named his book *The Man with Total Control*, a strange story about a recluse who never left his room, forever guarding the borders of his universe. The character's name was Jeremy Mueller and this was his secret journal, undoubtedly found well past his death.

John began to read into the depths of his book, words of deep meaning darting from the pages.

*Suddenly, the forest became totally quiet . . .*

21

*no movement, no breath. The magician twitched, raising stiff fingers as a signal of possible alarm. We stopped.*

*Far down the tunneled clearing, a monstrous white tiger with large hollow eyes stared silently. I had seen those eyes before, yet they were blank.*

*The tiger began its charge. The magician yelled at me to run, escape. I looked toward him for an instant as he dove headlong into the center of the icy lake, his only option to drown.*

*I tried to move, but my body would not react to my raging mind, paralyzed into the white tiger's charge. His speed, grace, power overwhelmed the snow. Only my feet had reached water as the gigantic beast caught me, entrapped me, the full force of its charge around me, yet did not harm me, only held me . . . then, I awoke.*

*It was a false warning.*

Certainly, the book still had impact. So why, John thought, was it stored with rubble? By now, the novel should have been in its ninth or tenth printing. It should be required reading in universities across the nation. Both intellectuals and the general public should agree that *The Man with Total Control* is one of the finest works of literature ever written. Hemingway, Faulkner, Steinbeck . . . Hammond.

"And not David," John muttered to himself.

Why had this not happened?

As frustration began to mix with anger, John stalled on another passage.

*Soft beside a whirlwind, a man was primed to dance.*

# THE BRAVE HISTORIAN

*He claimed to understand the movements, though his body appeared motionless.*

As always, John tried to storm past the two-sentence paragraph, momentarily pretending it was written by someone of great significance, someone other than him, someone who was not revealing the tragically bungled story of his own life. No, it was just fiction; not about a real person, not about John.

No movement.

Same with this other book he was pretending to write. *The Brave Historian* could also be a masterpiece if he would ever finish and then somehow manage to get it published by somebody, anybody.

"It's Robert Patterson's fault," John mumbled to himself. "He has got to be more . . ."

John stopped, not needing to complete the thought. Okay, Patterson was so pounded and stale that he no longer bothered to fight. But the main character cannot be weak.

If John were to write Patterson making love with a beautiful woman, would it include an apology?

"Hey, I was once strong, but now I am just a lonely historian who has lost the sun. Can I arouse you with my poems?"

John winced, trying to strangle his pen.

"Ain't nobody gonna sleep with a scared man," John angrily blurted to his empty room.

John paused, purposely attempting to change course. He took a deep breath.

Retract the blame. It is not the fault of Robert Patterson. How can you place responsibility on someone who is nothing more than a fictional image?

Well, for certain he needed to change Patterson's name. Something slightly foreign, but still American, with a bit of mystery. What the hell did this have to do with creativity?

"You've got to have a gimmick these days," John stated out loud to himself for probably the one-thousandth time, as if the ultimate rule of fiction was that "normal names don't work and historians are boring."

What was he saying? John stopped talking to himself and once again rolled the plot and words of *The Brave Historian* through his tired mind. There was nothing wrong with the idea, nothing wrong with the words, nothing wrong with historians. In fact, the book did have spark and meaning. And even Robert Patterson was fine. Perhaps fix him up with a quick injection of testosterone.

John just needed one more round of edits, a few new ideas.

The good news was that a good number of his books were near completion—*Pirate Ships, The Last Living Child of India, The Man with Total Control, 1945, Go Down West Virginia.*

What really mattered, John once again envisioned, was that any of these novels could have been his ticket to fame and glory. They would have opened a life of opportunity, creativity and big bucks.

Or perhaps nothing at all.

Trapped at the outer edge of the fire, John could no longer feel its warmth. You see, he had never shown his writings to anyone. Not friends, not relatives, not literary agents, not publishers. Like himself, his stories remained unknown.

Of course, there was always a reason. It needed more work. He wasn't sure where to send it. Maybe it wasn't really that good after all. What if it was rejected? Besides, he was uneasy with the sales pitch. The business appeared to be so complex. Should he just walk into a publisher's office and ask to speak with an editor? Aren't you supposed to have an agent?

Plus, it was always too soon to make a proposal. The words

were not yet perfect. He just needed the right atmosphere to create. He just needed to add a few more finishing touches. He just needed more time.

And it probably didn't matter the quality of the work, because he had always heard that getting published was a million-to-one shot. It was the old "you're nothing until you're something" rule.

John realized it made no sense for him to be bitter. Despite the millions of fools who had somehow landed ahead of him in life, there were probably just as many brilliant people forever wading in trenches.

For now, fame would have to be put on hold.

Ah, the excuses a dreamer can fashion.

"Idiot," he whispered.

Undoubtedly, there were thousands of obscure writers having produced works that were deep, tender, different, unpublished, unread. So, they locked their extraordinary manuscripts in a secret vault, much like Jeremy Mueller, *The Man with Total Control*, might guard his very existence.

> *I perceived myself as the tragic artist. Van Gogh, Kafka . . . amazing depth, perception, beauty. And yet dead, with no paintings sold and instructions for the writings to be cremated.*

\* \* \* \*

Thanksgiving 1999. The California fall was pretending to kick, the chill keeping John from his daily walk. Two days had passed since he'd ventured outdoors and he was restless.

Daniel and Katherine Stroud's house was warm with the season, the smell of a feast, the Detroit Lions and Chicago Bears battling on the TV. John looked around the living room, jammed with assorted friends and Katherine's relatives, searching for someone he might recognize.

John had been a friend of Daniel forever, but these people were strangers. Then again, he'd only lived with the Stroud family for several months. Katherine had probably never told her relatives about this 99-year-old man her husband had decided to invite into the heart of the family.

John moved closer to the TV, hoping to find sanctuary in the game. He was blocked.

"Hey John," said Zack. "This is my cousin Jimmy, he's 12, but I got him beat by three months."

John put out his hand to shake, but Jimmy just stared, and then asked, "How old are you?"

"Well," said John, "if you are 12, I've got you by almost 88 years."

While Jimmy was attempting the math, Zack continued the introduction.

"John was a sportswriter and he talked to Babe Ruth and he knows a whole bunch of dead Hall of Famers. Tell him, John."

"Okay, have you heard of Lou Gehrig?"

"Nope," said Jimmy.

"Christy Mathewson?"

"Nope."

"How about Ted Williams?"

"Um, maybe."

"But you have heard of Babe Ruth?"

"The fat guy on the Yankees who hit all the home runs."

"Babe wasn't always rotund," said John.

Jimmy's interest was fading.

"I like football better," he said.

"John knows dead football players too," said Zack. "He knew the Galloping Ghost. John, tell him about that guy."

"Jimmy, you ever heard of Red Grange?"

"Nope."

"Jim Thorpe?"

"Nope."

"Well, who do you like in today's game, Bears or Lions?"

"I guess I like the Bears," said Jimmy, "but my favorite teams are the Raiders and Cowboys."

"John and I like the Chargers," said Zack. "Which means we hate the Raiders and could kick your Cowboy butts."

"You're crazy," argued Jimmy, "we got Troy Aikman and Emmitt Smith and Neon Deon Sanders."

"Big deal," said Zack. "Junior Seau can wipe the field with all three of them."

"No way," yelled Jimmy. "C'mon, let's go outside and play some football. I'll be the Cowboys and you're the Chargers."

"You are toast," said Zack.

And they were gone.

It would prove to be the most interesting conversation of the day.

John spotted an empty chair near the game, noticing that the Lions were winning. But as he began his walk, Daniel grabbed his arm.

"John, let me introduce you to a few folks."

John wanted to decline, but had no retreat.

"Bill and Linda," Daniel said to a middle-aged couple, "I want you to meet my good friend John Hammond."

"Nice to meet you John," said Bill, his wife adding a pleasant nod.

"Bill's my cousin from Pasadena," said Daniel.

"Been there," said John. "It was about 1927 or so, a beautiful little town."

"Well, now it's big," laughed Bill. "Still beautiful in many places, but basically a jam-packed city."

"John lives in our guest room," said Daniel. "In a month, he's going to have his 100th birthday."

"You don't look a hundred," said Bill.

And so it went . . .

The relatives were surprised to learn of John's age, but even more shocked that he was living in the house. It came with the usual assortment of whispers and stares.

"I hope the old guy makes it through dinner," joked Katherine's brother when John was out of the room. "When I hit that age, just take me out to the pasture and shoot me."

The return laughter was guarded and uneasy, as if everyone realized the comment had been inappropriate. Then again, nobody exactly stood up for John's right to be ancient.

"John's a nice man," Katherine replied to her brother, "He's interesting, he's thoughtful, and if you'd like him to visit your house for a while, I'm sure we can work something out."

Daniel glanced sternly at his wife, then looked away, pretending not to hear.

Katherine didn't push. The discussion had run its course many times over.

\* \* \* \*

Alone in the study, John could hear the celebration from the living room. He considered rejoining them, but the comfort of his chair was too powerful.

And now his body felt very heavy, his eyes quite tired, his mind beginning to drift. It was soft, warm.

\* \* \* \*

In the dream, John Hammond returned to his childhood. It

was a Pennsylvania fall, leaves glistening streaks of gold and red, sky the deepest blue, air warm with the slight sting of a crisp breeze.

Father was young and laughing, playing tag with David. Mary was building a castle in the mud, mother sitting in the orchard and humming a gentle tune. Hers was a song about a family that lasted forever. It had always been one of John's favorites and he wished she would sing just a little louder, but the words seemed muffled.

Mother was still so beautiful, he thought, after all these years. Perhaps he had been mistaken, perhaps he only thought she was dead.

She was pleased to see him again.

"Look, everybody," she said, "Johnny has come home."

Everyone gathered around him.

David put his arm on John's shoulder; Mary smiled and gently touched his cheek.

"Our family is back together," said father. "What took you so long to get here, son?"

And then he held the boy tightly.

John started to back away, but was caught by the strength of his father's arms.

"We need to finally talk," George Hammond whispered, pulling him closer. "We can be friends again."

That would be nice, thought John. He tried to gulp, but emotion took charge as tears began to form. So strange this warmth. His body was strong, his soul recharged.

Suddenly, the family turned quiet. He could hear a rustling from behind. He turned quickly to the sound, then plunged into slow motion.

There they were, the most wonderful sight he had ever seen. His heart flowed, his throat choked. He couldn't swallow, he couldn't move.

The two Sarahs standing together, holding hands and smiling. His little sister, his precious daughter.

Was this possible? Hints of hope and wonder stormed through his mind, but all thought was lost. He just needed his daughter to hug and hold, to keep forever.

He rushed toward the little girls. He would not wait, he would not falter. He had never moved faster.

"Johnny," shouted his little sister.

"Daddy, daddy," cried his baby daughter.

And now they were both so close, so close . . .

He awoke in a cold, sticky sweat. Reality struck like a raging ocean ever pounding the ravaged shore. Wait, he had to go back. He quickly closed his eyes. He pretended to never have awakened. He searched, he pleaded.

But they were gone.

\* \* \* \*

John's mind began to shake, tearing his body away from a now distant dream. He closed his eyes again, desperate to return. No chance, it was gone, forever lodged into the past.

He could hear music coming from the living room. Kids were playing, parents were laughing.

# CHAPTER 3

Shelly Kingston was jogging on the beach, running south toward the cliffs of Torrey Pines. The sun seemed warm for early December, the smell of the ocean breeze and dying seaweed engaging all of her senses. What more could she want? Sure, there were way too many people in Southern California and it was time-consuming traveling the 15 miles from Del Mar to San Diego, but living a block from the Pacific Ocean certainly had its advantages; especially on days like this, when she was virtually alone with her body and thoughts.

She was thinking, as she ran, about how many movies she had seen during her lifetime. A thousand? Should she count the ones she had seen more than five or six times—*Raiders of the Lost Ark, One Flew Over the Cuckoo's Nest, Somewhere in Time, Titanic?* Her mom and dad went back to *Casablanca, Rear Window, Tom Jones, Lawrence of Arabia, Easy Rider.* They were the true movie fanatics who always included their only child. Comedies, musicals, love stories, animation, westerns—she had probably seen several hundred movies by the time she entered kindergarten.

Shelly continued to run strong on the wet sand, a smile emerging as she recalled the occasional R-rated movie when Mom would cough and Dad would cover her eyes during the more delicate scenes. It's good to love your mom and dad, she thought.

An independent filmmaker, Shelly cringed at the thought of still living in her parents' home. It was embarrassing. "Don't look at it like that," her dad had said. "This way, Sweetheart, you can save money and afford to be your own boss."

They also had built her an office and studio at the side of the house. Yes, it was the smart way to start a business. But the real world was testing her now, she thought. Well, sort of. It was true that she did manage to spend much of the summer and a good portion of the cooler months on the beach, but that was for exercise and inspiration. She could easily find more work if the hunt wasn't so painful.

Besides, she had her own ideas about creating movies. She was always with her camera, plotting story lines and experimenting with angles and light. Spielberg, Hitchcock, Coppola; that's how all great filmmakers get their start. Okay, men were grabbing all the awards and there was tons of luck involved in breaking through to stardom, but you still had to have talent.

\* \* \* \*

Shelly was busy in her studio working on one of her original short films and dreaming of accepting an Academy Award. Lost in her editing, she was slightly startled by the knock on the door.

"Come on in, Dad," she hollered. She knew the knock.

"Hi Baby," he said. "Am I disturbing you?"

"No," she smiled, "I'm just finishing this short I've been working on."

"How are your finances progressing?" he asked, ever careful not to pop the creative balloon. He was, after all, her top critic and best fan.

"I've got a couple of projects that can get me through the month," she said. "But, seriously Dad, take a look at this piece I just finished. I did the shooting in one day, but I've spent most of the week editing. I think it might be the best thing I've ever done."

"Okay, break open the popcorn," he said, already intrigued. "I'm ready."

"I asked these two guys from San Diego State who are Native Americans to dress in these original garments they own," said Shelly. "Stick with me, this is like a gold mine."

"As in money?" her father said.

"No, as in ideas," she said, not even worrying that he might be more interested in the state of her checkbook.

"Look, I've got them walking through the forest. I've eliminated all sound except the softness of their steps. Are you watching?"

"Yes, yes," he said. "Quiet."

And the film took control.

*Two young warriors walk silently through the woods, perhaps hunting for food, perhaps exploring the boundaries of their lives. Ever focusing on the moment, they are deep within a forest of quiet sound and cautious reflex.*

"Do you feel the reality of this, Dad?" said Shelly.

"Let me watch," he whispered.

*One of the boys leans down to run the moist dirt through his fingers. He listens to the sound of distant birds as a soft wind rustles through trees and leaves. It is totally quiet but for the noise of life.*

33

"Nothing but life," Shelly commented, "you can even smell it."

Her dad put his finger to his mouth to quietly hush the child. He was already wrapped into the mood she had created.

*Suddenly, they both stop and listen. There is a feint sound in the far distance, something they have never heard before. It seems to be getting louder. This is not the sound of an animal or the wind or even a landslide. The earth begins to rumble with a slight shake as the noise becomes distinctly loud and powerful.*

*They share a look of concern. What could this be? They have no idea, but they must escape this place immediately. They run through the forest, the camera capturing their feet as they pound against the dead leaves and soil. They are swift as they tear through twigs and vines, now beginning to pant, now beginning to tire, but still pushing hard to escape this sound that is now beginning to overtake their very being.*

"Check this, Dad," says Shelly, "This is cool."
"Shelly, shush."

*The sound is deafening. Their feet continue to run through the land, but their bodies are exhausted, mind and nerves near paralyzed with panic. The sound is too loud, their power too weak, their movement too slow. Like an animal captured by death, their eyes and minds cannot accept this moment.*

34

*The camera pans back to their feet, the sprint no longer soft. They run, they struggle. And now there is a shockingly swift blur within the camera as the feet of these proud warriors move from forest to hard dirt to paved concrete. Flickering lights seem to appear in the background to clock their movement. What is this place? But there is no time to think, to realize. The monstrous sound is unbearable. They run. They try to escape. Their effort near collapse as they are suddenly consumed by what appears to be a large 707 airplane landing where stood life, but no more. And now the noise is different, the two warriors gone.*

"Unbelievable," said her dad.

His first thought was that Shelly needed to immediately package this work, to enter it into every film festival she could find. Properly marketed, this could be the key to a secure and high-paying career. That's what he wanted to say, but his heart kept him quiet. She was fortunate that he realized creativity and business were seldom an unblemished mix.

* * * *

As she awaited success with a green but growing portfolio, Shelly managed to attain a bit of money by putting together music videos for small-time artists also looking for a seam to stardom. In fact, she had just completed a breakthrough video for a group from Orange County called Living Hell. The quality and style of the film was easily good enough for MTV, except that the band was dreadful and their song, *Your Guts Suck*, was disgusting. On the other hand, the four Living Hell guys—two electric guitars, a drummer, and a screamer on lead vocals—believed they were great. They gladly paid Shelly the $12,000 invoice and ventured off to sell themselves to the highest bidder.

"This video is gonna crack it for us big-time," said Living Hell's lead singer, Bloodlust (alias Frank Jones), a smile turning his uniquely etched face into an amazing graphic. "Thanks Shelly, you the fuckin' bomb."

"You're welcome," she said.

At times the money was good, but always the costs were exorbitant. Still, she did okay with various freelance assignments, including NFL films. She also had a few local TV deals from stations with tight budgets and skeleton staffs.

Shelly wasn't quite desperate enough to be looking for a full-time job; unless it was Hollywood, unless it was motion pictures.

So, for now, documentaries and short films were her thing. That's how you begin. Searching for style and hoping for luck. Her works were both raw and interesting.

The kid had talent.

The kid was broke.

Fact is, Shelly produced much more than she sold. Mostly, she managed to work out the funding with her father. He'd listen and nod and agree. He was bound by love and had the cash anyway, so the payback was whenever and all she had to carry was a slight dose of self-inflicted guilt. By most artistic aspects, the burden was light.

Hey, she was restless for fame and big bucks. Just one good break would be all it would take. Surely, she was destined for the silver screen and that long line of Academy Awards.

Directed by Michelle R. Kingston.

She was 27 years old and had paid her dues. If only she could put her life into fast-forward.

# THE BRAVE HISTORIAN

\* \* \* \*

Shelly was sitting at her desk, glancing at the wall, a Star Wars poster next to her framed diploma—San Diego State University, Class of 1994. Looking out the window, she noticed a lone seagull perched on the fence at the far side of the yard, seemingly oblivious that late November had turned somewhat dreary. Furthermore, the idiot bird acted as if he owned the place, treating both the patio and now ugly-covered swimming pool as a private dumping ground.

Back to work, Shelly noticed she had two messages on her telephone.

"Yo Shelly, this is Bloodlust from Living Hell. How you doin' pretty girl? Love the video, watch it every day. What's happening is we've been working on some new songs and are looking to raise some cash to make a new album. Didn't know it cost so much to become famous, hah. Anyway, I was wondering if you would be a dear girl and hold onto that check we gave you for maybe a couple more weeks, tops."

Shaking her head, Shelly prematurely erased the remainder of the tape.

"Sorry," she announced to the empty room, "too late."

Were these guys crazy? She laughed. She had cashed that check nearly a month ago. In fact, she had gone to the bank that very afternoon and it had cleared exactly five working days later, to great relief.

Second voice message:

"Hello, Ms. Kingston, my name is Daniel Stroud. I was told you were an outstanding filmmaker and I would possibly like to hire you to make a short and personal documentary of a friend of mine who will soon be celebrating his 100th birthday. I'll call back later to check on your availability and rates. Thanks."

37

Shelly wrote down the name and erased the message. Another brainless assignment; the kind you do in a few hours, then take twice as long splicing and writing a couple of catchy one-liners to attract attention for a patterned 15-minute production.

She had done her share of these things, always with reluctance. Really, they were easy. She would just make up the questions as the interview was rolling. Maybe it would be interesting, probably not. Whatever, she'd do the piece and hope the next project would be a bit more relevant.

Okay, this is about an old man turning 100. Great, another damn visit to the rest home. She hated these things.

\* \* \* \*

Daniel Stroud called again the next morning, introducing himself as a high school English teacher from North San Diego County.

"I have a close friend of the family who, come January, will have lived in three centuries," he said with a strange hint of pride. "I'd like to get some of his character and history professionally documented. And I just didn't want to grab a camcorder, you know, and have it turn into a drab never-leave-the-couch video. Because, really, he's extremely interesting."

It sounded simple enough. Reaching for a pen and paper, Shelly politely asked for some background.

"Sure," said Daniel, "my friend, John Hammond, was born just before midnight on the last day of 1899. John's father, George Hammond, was the famous composer way back when, his sister Mary the artist, and brother David the writer. You've no doubt heard of the Hammond Family."

"Well, maybe," replied Shelly. "Wait, I read a novel by

38

David Hammond when I was in college. It was called *Blue* something. *Blue Gold*; that was it, *Blue Gold*. Really bizarre. Easily the most unsettling book I have ever read. That was probably the same guy."

"Yep, that was definitely the same David Hammond," said Daniel. "I'm afraid his brother John was not one of the famous Hammonds, but he was a sportswriter for a number of newspapers until he retired about thirty years ago. He's helped me out on many occasions in my classes. He's well-schooled in journalism, creative writing, history and a number of other subjects, including the art of storytelling. When he's feeling good, he can spin a yarn like nobody I have ever heard."

"What's he like?" Shelly asked.

"He's a character," said Daniel. "He has a great sense of humor, but can be moody. I'm guessing that comes with his age."

"What about family?" she asked. "Will we be including any of them?"

"No," he said, "I think they're all dead. I know he was married and had a child, but he's very quiet about those things. He doesn't talk about them at all. Maybe if you could get him to open up a bit about his family and other people in his life, that's one of the things that would be good to capture on film."

Excellent, thought Shelly, I'll be interviewing a man with no future who doesn't like to talk about the past.

"One other thing that would probably work well for the video," added Daniel. "John plays the piano. It's his own stuff and very original."

Shelly tried to hold back a giggle, an idea popping in her head of a music documentary featuring old John Hammond rocking out with Bloodlust. She regained her composure.

"Interesting," she said.

"Usually he claims his back and hands hurt too much to play," continued Daniel, "but I don't buy it. I've heard him playing when he thinks the house is empty. The music is very beautiful. To tell the truth, I've never heard anything quite like it."

"He lives with you?"

"Well, with me and my family," said Daniel. "I have a wife and two kids. We live in Escondido."

A good thirty minutes to the east, thought Shelly, who had a tendency to calculate every geographical location in relationship to the Pacific Ocean.

"We've had him stay with us the past few months," Daniel continued. "It's a little difficult, but he's very capable and we're not worried that he'll burn the house down or leave his medicines on the counter or anything like that, knock on wood."

Shelly could hear Daniel tapping the top of a desk.

"I have known John my entire life," he continued. "He was my grandfather's best friend and often took care of me when I was growing up. Plus, John and I are writing a book. Well, he's writing and I'm editing."

"He writes too?"

"Well, when he came to live with us, the shipment included about three dozen large cardboard boxes filled with notebooks and notes and scribblings that he had accumulated. Beyond the stuff he wrote for newspapers, I don't think anything has ever been published."

"Maybe it's not that good," said Shelly, immediately wondering why she'd say such a thing considering she didn't even know the man.

"Oh, it's good," said Daniel. "He's exceptional."

"What's your book about?"

"It's sort of a history of the twentieth century, but it's not at all about major events. John always reminds me that it's not about history at all. I'd say it's about moments and feelings and how life is totally unexplainable. It's really hard to talk about because it's very unique. If anything, we're kind of attacking history from a totally different angle, unfolding through the eyes and mind of a history teacher who realizes that what he has studied and taught is quite meaningless and that everything around him has sort of snowballed out of control. I'm sorry, I don't always explain it as well as I should, which can be a problem, particularly since I'm supposed to be the editor of the book."

"What's the book called?"

"We're thinking about calling it *The Brave Historian*. But, I don't know, you always want a title that will sell a million books; so if we can think of something clever, bingo."

"I like the title," said Shelly. "How close are you to completion?"

"Well, we do have a good number of pages," he said, "but we're a long way from finished. To be truthful, John is constantly rethinking and restructuring the content. It seems like he's always working on another draft. It gets frustrating."

Daniel stopped, realizing that he shouldn't be mentioning any behind-the-scenes details to Shelly.

"Is that mainly what he writes about?" asked Shelly. "History?"

"No, like I said, it's not so much about history as a perception of the past and its consequences to the present," said Daniel. "But I probably should be careful with definitions because his writing can be deceptive. He's kind of unusual."

"What do you mean?"

"Well, I wouldn't want you to tell him," said Daniel, his voice trailing into a sound of secrecy. "This is totally off the record, but I've peaked into some of the boxes he has stored at my home. Some of it is just random thoughts and personal history.

Evidently, he occasionally kept a diary over the course of his lifetime. But there also seems to be a lot of fiction. And, I'll tell you something, his structure is a little out of the ordinary, but some of his plots can turn really deep. The words and meanings have an almost uneasy intensity. In my opinion, I would even say that some of it is absolutely brilliant."

"May I ask why you want this documentary filmed?"

"Well, think about it," said Daniel. "John has lived every single moment of the 20th century and at least specks of both the 19th and soon the 21st. He comes from a famous family, even though he never mentions any of them. He's very creative and, I think, somewhat peculiar, in a good way. I just figured, the way things work in this world that it might be important to have him on film. He's old. He's not going to last forever."

Shelly was half listening, still thinking about the possibilities surrounding John's writings.

"Why do you suppose he's never been published?" she asked.

"I don't know. Like I told you, he's very elusive about some things. Maybe he'll tell you, maybe not. I will say that he does seem to have his secrets, but there are some things he just never cares to discuss. It's only an opinion, but from being around him, I think there are instances in his past he never talks about because he's somewhat haunted by them."

Secrets?

It wasn't necessarily the challenge that struck Shelly's imagination, but the unknown. What kind of secrets? And what exactly was inside those boxes of words? For all she knew, John Hammond might be the greatest writer of the century, a 99-year-old genius somehow undiscovered.

Long after hanging up the phone, she was still wrapped into Daniel Stroud's description of the old man. If it was true what he said about John Hammond, she could be stumbling into the turning point of her film career. Her senses were stimulated, her creative juices boiling beneath a mind exploding with new possibilities.

Writers are sometimes stormy or reclusive or grumpy, she knew that. But beneath the turmoil, a writer might also be sensitive and deep. This could be a connection that might forever influence her life.

On the other hand, it could be absolutely nothing.

And if the thing was going to be a bust, Shelly might as well call Daniel Stroud back and turn the project down. Except that she needed the work, needed the money.

\* \* \* \*

Shelly headed for Daniel Stroud's home in Escondido. Despite Led Zeppelin's *Stairway to Heaven* blaring on her radio, she was feeling uneasy and somewhat unprepared.

It was Saturday, December 4, 1999, rather bleak and cold for this time of year. In fact, the last day of sun had been a few days after Thanksgiving. This had to be some sort of record for hideous weather. Like all true Southern Californians when denied their daily dose of sunshine, Shelly was feeling gloomy, a touch suicidal, as if the sun might never shine again.

That would be a great idea for a movie, she thought. A strange fog comes ashore at Laguna Beach, leading to public panic as thousands of Californians kill themselves because of a prediction by a famed surfer/guru that the sun is forever gone. They jump out of buildings, run naked on the San Diego Freeway, ram hang gliders into Sunset Cliffs, bash their surf boards into jet skis or their jet skis into Naval aircraft carriers, ingest various killer drug sampler plates.

Hundreds invade Malibu in an attempt to break the *Guin-*

43

*ness Book of World Records* for mass suicide. Holding hands, they walk into the water never to return. Some wear wet suits.

This would be Southern California at its most bizarre, millions joining the extravaganza, each attempting a more dramatic and creative death.

She could get Bloodlust to do a cameo, putting Living Hell's *Your Guts Suck* on the soundtrack. Why not get all of the Living Hell boys in the movie? They'd all have to die, but talk about type-casting, they'd love it.

In fact, instead of a killer fog doing away with half the state, an even better idea would be to alter the plot so anyone who hears *Your Guts Suck* turns insane within 24 hours, the very sound of Living Hell causing a deadly pulse to pass through the ear canal into the brain, eyes of the victims turning a putrid green as the sun vanishes from their sight. What would start as a twitch would progress to a maddened brain thumping its way toward self-destruction.

Yes, that makes much more sense.

It would be a B-movie, an instant cult classic. Then, when the last fool had died, the sun would reappear and Californians would return to the beach; except now there would be a lot more room.

All she would need is a short proposal and a working title. How about calling it *The Worst Movie Ever to Be Rejected by All of Hollywood and for Good Reason?*

"Time out," Shelly blurted above Led Zeppelin, momentarily turning the radio down, then back to three-quarters blast. She loved this song.

But it was time to focus on her real project, the old man's birthday.

On further thought, Shelly wondered if Mr. Stroud's description of John Hammond might have been nothing more than a great exaggeration. He had built up the old man as some sort of famous undiscovered writer of the future. Or was he a piano-playing sportswriter of the past? Who knew?

Most likely Daniel Stroud just wanted a keepsake of the old man before he died.

Really, it didn't matter. Shelly had her own problems. First was a long-planted apprehension of heading into unfamiliar surroundings, hardly the mark of a true filmmaker. She also didn't necessarily enjoy being around old people. They made her nervous. What do you talk about? Can they even hear you? Are their minds working correctly?

And just to be real, the thought of dealing with an uncooperative old goat further ruined this lousy day.

She took a deep breath to calm her nerves. "Relax," she said to herself, "I can do this."

Her mind eased, Led Zeppelin taking control as Shelly altered her vocal chords into a high-pitched frenzy.

*And as I walk on down the road.*

Okay, she'd keep it light, shoot some film while asking a few questions and then leave. If there were no better offers between now and then, she could return for a final shooting on New Year's Eve, record the exact moment the old man turned 100, provided he was still alive.

That was the plan.

She had no idea that John Hammond would be quite so fascinating.

\* \* \* \*

Daniel Stroud met Shelly at the door of his Escondido home, explaining that John might be a bit cranky. He was not pleased at the idea of starring in his own video.

GAINES

"It's too late now," Daniel had said to John. "She's going to be here in half an hour, so just try to cooperate. Here's a new shirt I bought for you. They say you should wear bright colors, but not blue. And you shouldn't wear thin stripes."

"What do I care what I look like?" growled John. "This is ridiculous."

"No, I want to document some of your life. Just think of it as a lesson in history. Geez, John, who else has been alive for the whole century? Plus, when we complete our book, this piece of film will be something for future generations to appreciate."

"It'll be something for the garbage can," John grumbled, "because I'm just not in the mood right now to talk about my dashing journey through the past 100 years. I'm tired, and right now I can't remember a damn thing except that I'm ticked at you for pulling such an idiotic prank. You didn't even ask. Maybe I'm too busy. I should call a lawyer and kick your butt out of my will, all 25 bucks."

"Just take a deep breath, John, and give it a chance. All I ask is that you meet the girl. Her name is Shelly Kingston. She seems very talented."

"Shelly Kingston? What, Steven Spielberg turn you down?"

"That's the spirit," said Daniel. "Just be your usual snappy self. Have some fun with this thing."

Well, it wasn't as if John had anything else to do that day, so he grumbled some more and put on the new shirt, first removing the price tag.

"Thirty bucks for a shirt?" he griped. "Has the world gone mad?"

He looked in the mirror. Very stylish, he thought. Yeah, he looked pretty good in dark tan. Then again, he used to look a lot better.

\* \* \* \*

46

While Daniel was gathering John, Shelly returned to her van for the usual three trips of rolling and lugging all the film equipment, a process apparently designed for a weightlifter.

Back in the house, she studied the room, the shadows and light.

As she began to set up, Daniel returned.

"You have a beautiful home," she said to him.

"Thank you, my wife has a great eye for decorating. She's out with the kids right now. They wanted to stay and watch, but we figured you might not need any background disruptions."

"No problem," Shelly said with a smile, wondering what his wife and children might look like. He was fairly handsome for a man in probably his mid-forties or later; hard to tell.

"John is making progress," said Daniel. "These things can be productions."

Shelly continued the assembly.

"You sure have a lot of equipment," said Daniel, suddenly self-conscious that his comment might be misunderstood. But she does, he thought to himself.

"Is there anything you need?" he continued, feeling the flush in his face.

"No, I'm nearly ready. I have some ideas, but they're sort of predicated on the subject. It might be best to simply jump into the interview and see what develops."

"Good," said Daniel, "I'll go back and try to hurry our star."

Shelly's mind was transfixed on the operation. Too bad she didn't have a film crew, she thought. She could have used somebody to unload all of the equipment, somebody to hold the microphone, a couple of cameras going at the same time. Some day.

Just then, John Hammond appeared, a cane slightly helping his balance. Shelly immediately found his eyes and smiled.

John tried to pull his eyes away, but couldn't. There was something very familiar, very striking about her.

Was his mind deceiving him? He squinted, stared; he was stunned. Jessica, it was Jessica. How could it be?

Well, it couldn't. Jessica had been dead for 50 years. This was just a remarkable resemblance. And, sure, there were differences. This was not Jessica, not a ghost, just a coincidence.

Wake up idiot, John's mind silently commanded. Of course it's not Jessica. Just the same, he realized he was staring. Sorry, he couldn't help himself. She was beautiful.

This was all happening in a matter of seconds, but the bombardment was total. He was struck by her beauty, her youth, her smile. She did not carry the powerful or striking features that might frighten the average man. Hers was not a harsh or chiseled beauty.

His body tensed, quivered. Inside, there was a gigantic gulp that seemed to start in the pit of his belly and zoom straight to the heart of his neck, trying to escape through a mouth dried by emotion. Then, without hesitation, the exotically peculiar feeling once again burst back to the depths of his stomach.

How long had it been since he felt such a jolt of passion? In all his life, he had only seen such beauty once, Jessica.

Shelly did not seem to realize that John's insides were uncontrollably clanging, his frazzled existence on full alert.

She approached him almost cautiously, wondering if anything might break. He did not notice the hesitation.

John had planned to fight this interview, to be angry and aloof. Forget that.

"I'm John Hammond," he said, extending his right hand. "It's a pleasure to meet you, Shelly."

They touched hands, Shelly returning the introductory compliments to an old man who was suddenly realizing that his smile was beginning to hurt his face.

"I was born 70 years too soon," he heard himself mutter. What a stooge, he thought. Why did I say that? Seventy years too soon? Why not just ask her to go dancing on Saturday night?

Okay, spoken words had never been his strength. He did have a tendency to fumble, but how crude and chauvinistic that remark must have sounded to her.

Actually, Shelly took it as an old man's compliment, nothing more.

"I'm very much looking forward to working with you," she said. "I think the first step should just be to roll the camera, start talking and see where it takes us."

John could hear her words, but was more entranced with the tone of her voice. It was soft, yet clear and smooth.

Funny, but for such a long time, John had not paid much attention to the beauty of a woman. That entire feeling that had at times consumed his younger life had instantly returned—the thought pattern, the vitality, the sexual wonder.

Sure, there were those TV commercials with Super Models 75 percent naked, now an accepted reminder that somewhere along the line he had become a relic. Young and beautiful women had long looked away as if his presence was of no concern, so why should he care about them? Or something like that.

But, great balls of fire, this was different. There was a look and fragrance about this girl that seemed to roar across his body, igniting a feeling that had been absent for years. For a moment, he felt somewhat young. For just a moment, and then it faded.

He clutched his cane. How silly, he thought, how wonderful.

49

# CHAPTER 4

The first shoot was somewhat awkward.

John would have been more comfortable with just Shelly, but the damn camera seemed like a third party ever butting into the conversation.

"Just pretend the camera isn't there," said Shelly.

John looked into the lens and wrinkled his face.

"Go away," he said. "I mean it, camera, you're a pest."

Shelly smiled.

"While I'm complaining," he said, "isn't the lighting just a bit intense? I might need some serious makeup."

John moved forward, staring into the eye of the camera.

"I didn't do it, Rocky. I tell you, I didn't do it," he said with a voice right out of a 1940s gangster movie. "It was her, all along. It was her, I tell you. I was just following orders. Look at her, Rocky. What was I to do?"

"James Cagney," laughed Shelly.

"A pathetic Cagney," inserted John. "I would think he would be too old for you."

"No, I'm a big movie fan," said Shelly, realizing that this could be a fun interview.

John was thinking the same thing. Who cared if the camera was right in his face? This woman was worth the intrusion.

And it was more than restlessness he felt. There was a yearn-ing, he was sure of that.

She was so young, so vibrant, so alive; and so much like Jessica. God, how deeply he had once loved that woman.

He tried to ignore the obvious comparisons, but couldn't. The way she walked, smiled, talked, even smelled were all so familiar. Her face, her beauty.

Wait, what the hell was happening? He had known this girl less than 15 minutes, and was now obsessing over the impossible? Slow down old man. He needed to regain some sensibility, but was too weak to fight it off.

John felt a distant surge to touch her. But, of course, he didn't.

\* \* \* \*

They talked for nearly two hours, Shelly eventually securing the large camera on a tripod. John seemed to dance across the century with stories about his youth, his friends, his dreams.

"When I was a young boy, I clearly remember charting my entire life," he said. "With much thought, I had selected professional baseball to be my career. I would play for the New York Giants, so I could team with my idol, Christy Mathewson. He'd be old and I'd be young, but we'd be the best pitching duo in baseball.

"I'd also play until I was too old to throw, honorably giving my position on the Giants to a young rookie in need of a chance. After all, I could live on my glory, young kids asking me to recall the string of no-hitters and World Series victories. I'd just tell them I always tried my best and was lucky to be the greatest pitcher in history. Well, me and Matty."

John stretched in his chair, seemingly adjusting his pitching arm and, at the same time, attempting to crack his backbones into place.

"And then after baseball," he continued, "I would play the piano and paint western landscapes, soaking the canvas with the colors and peculiarly soft feeling of an Arizona sunrise. You know, you're so tired and yet you have just awakened to the beauty of a moment and place that engulfs your mind and body with an amazing strength. There is a warmth and energy you swear can open a crease to life's every question and answer."

He tried again to stretch his back.

"I always wanted to be wild," he added, "but I was too quiet. I was going to be a major league baseball player, but I never tried. As for playing the piano, painting, writing."

John smiled ever so faintly, then continued.

"As a child, I didn't realize the energy would eventually so completely evaporate."

\* \* \* \*

Shelly found John Hammond to be a kind and remarkable person. He didn't look 99 and certainly didn't act his age. Sure, he was old, but not as frail or exhausted as she might have expected. He didn't even shake all that much. She also had figured his mind would be weak and wandering, damaged by time. But he had a certain flair. He was fun, warm and somewhat of a rebel.

And they had hit it off instantly.

A man who kept secrets? John seemed willing to talk about anything. His demeanor was not even close to Daniel Stroud's glum description. The old man had wit and spark and just the right amount of childish charm.

She had no idea what John was really thinking.

\* \* \* \*

John talked at length about the thrill and disaster of writing. It was a subject he addressed with great intensity.

"Have you ever seen the movie, Doctor Zhivago?" he asked.

"About a dozen times," Shelly responded.

"There's this one scene in the dead of winter," he continued. "It's deep into the night, cloaked with stillness, when the body has retreated and the brain is left alone to bolt uncharted paths. And, there, as starving wolves gather outside the walls of his snow-bound bungalow, Zhivago composes his poems to Lara."

John's long, frail fingers twitched, but his eyes seemed oddly young and expressive.

"To Zhivago, the surroundings are soft, almost hollow. He has no concern for the harsh cold, no fear as danger edges closer to the dim light of his one candle. For here is the center of the universe. On these grounds, the composer does thrive. The mind has found unlimited space. Words and meanings demolish all boundaries with passion and truth."

Shelly was stunned by the depth and intensity of John's words. Most people, cloaked by formalities, would dare not speak with such poetic grace.

"Have you ever had anything published?" Shelly asked, already aware of the answer.

"Ah, the life of a published author," he replied, taking a stab at portraying an expert. "Each novel seems to have its own separate existence with characters that invade the writer's mind until they are like old friends."

But the writing of each book was also touched by a familiar story that John did not mention to Shelly; the process of his writing in which all progress was eventually wasted. There were, naturally, the initial ideas and thoughts, followed by days of promise when the project was all that mattered in John's life. But then, always the plunge, weeks and months when every word was seemingly forgotten. Sometimes the writing came back, but it was always unfinished, always discarded.

There would be a time, he silently told himself, when he would be a complete and successful writer, when he would finally kick the fear of failure.

"Actually, I wrote a book back in the early '50s called *The Man with Total Control*," said John. "I finished it, did several rewrites through the years and finished it again. And then I tossed the manuscript in a box as if no one would possibly be interested in a story about a man who never left his room."

"When did you decide you wanted to be a writer?" Shelly asked, immediately realizing that she should have let him continue his thought.

"I've been writing since I was a kid, but I was about 25 when I started taking it seriously. Goodness, that's 75 years ago.

"I had already been writing sports for a small newspaper in Pennsylvania, but I wanted to write a novel. It was an exciting prospect, until I questioned why anyone would want to read something by an author who was too young. I know, my reasoning made little sense."

"I sense," said Shelly, "that you have written other books?" John turned his head, his eyes staring downward, processing her question.

How many books had he written? It had to be at least a dozen, he thought. Let's see, *The Man with Total Control* was done, although it could probably use another edit. And the same for *Chin Music*. A bunch were almost done—*The Last Living Man of India, 1945, Go Down West Virginia*. What were the others? John's mind was oddly blank for a moment, then twisting to the realization that he had no idea what he was trying to remember.

*Pirate Ships*, of course, and there were other books as well, but now he had lost interest.

Certainly, he continued to ponder, it was still possible to have these books published, but time was running out. Then again, he could be discovered and published after he was already dead. Considering all he had written, there was that distinct possibility.

Or maybe he should just light a match to all of it. Toss every word he had ever written in a dumpster. Well, some of it, maybe the junk. But not all of it. Not the good stuff.

John blinked. Where was he? Oh, the interview. His focus returned to the camera.

"You would think there would be room for one more great talent," he said, a trace of bitterness pushing at his voice. "You would think, and hope, and wonder if it's ever going to happen.

"I guess I always figured that next week I'd chart a plan; next year I'd be famous."

He stopped, eyes moving from the camera to Shelly and back again.

"Sorry," he said, "the answer is no, I've never published; unless you count 15,000 newspaper articles. I keep telling myself that my books are in various stages of completion. But all of them just sit—unpublished, unread, unimportant."

"Why?" she asked.

"I just never carried it to the next step, I suppose. I never made the effort to find a literary agent or publisher. I thought about it, but I just never really tried. I'm not sure if I was shy or stupid, or maybe both."

"Daniel told me about a new book," said Shelly. "Do you have plans for that?"

"I suppose it would not be impossible for *The Brave Historian* to be published, to be successful," said John. "A good publisher, a couple of breaks, the word spreads and it sells a million copies. I'd be the oldest rookie author in history."

\* \* \* \*

John also tossed around some stray ideas about music.

"Some people can sit down at the piano, stare at the sheet music and put the notes right into their hands," he said. "That's never worked for me. For the music to be felt, it must start at my fingers, not end there. The mind should be tuned into the soul, not entranced by some sheet of paper with notes splashed across treble clefs and measures. To be truly creative, you should play the music by instinct. My philosophy is that notes should be an afterthought, proof that you were there."

This was a philosophy? What the hell was he talking about? He couldn't even read music. Surely, Shelly would realize the flaws in such a shallow argument.

"Then again," he quickly added, "I'm sure a million piano teachers would probably disagree with me; and that's not to mention the band instructors who would be totally ticked. To tell the truth, there were a few times I tried to learn how to read music, but I always gave up. You know, as a sign of creativity. That said, I suppose I was just looking for the easy path."

He spoke about World War I.

"The Great War; that's what we called it back then, never imagining it would need a number."

"What about you?" she asked.

"I was thrown into it—too young, too frightened. We crossed the Atlantic, certain that the entire German Navy had marked our course. Their U-Boats were cold and silent monsters, ever stalking their prey. It was a blessing to finally escape the sea."

John silently scolded himself. Damn, he wasn't good at talking. At best, these sounded like descriptions from one of his old books. He was simply reading out loud the scribble from his mind.

Still, Shelly did not flinch. She seemed interested, so he continued this tale of what now seemed like another life, so distant as to almost feel like it had never happened at all.

"What we found was a ravaged land that boiled in the stench of mustard gas and death. I think we all tried to surround ourselves with powerful men who claimed to be brave, because most of us were just boys. We were vulnerable, scared, alone.

"It was best to be upwind and quiet, to have your rifle clean and loaded, to somehow survive, to somehow get home."

"What is your most vivid recollection of that time?" she asked.

John pulled back.

"On the day the war ended, we were jammed into a trench," he said quietly. "A kid named Chester Drums jumped up to cheer the news and a bullet hit him right in his face. We all shot back on reflex, but Chester just stood there, frozen in death, blood erupting from his head. Strange, but my first thought was anger at Chester for being so damn dumb."

John stopped, wondering about that one moment, his thoughts spiraling into ambiguity. Focus on the conversation, he told himself.

"Anyway, the war was over," he continued. "I just wanted to leave, to somehow not think about it at all."

But now he was back into the cloud that was stirring within his mind.

"To tell the truth, Shelly, distant memories sometimes become a bit unclear, even though it's easier nowadays for me to forget what happened five minutes ago."

John paused.

"I must apologize," he said, looking directly into Shelly's

57

eyes. "I'm afraid my mind has wandered. What I said about Chester Drums never happened."

He stopped again, took a deep breath that began strong but quickly wavered, then caught hold again.

"I was at sea when the Great War ended, riding a troop ship to Europe. We were the reinforcements that, fortunately, were never needed. Believe me, it was a great relief. I saw the devastation of war, but was never involved in an actual battle.

"And there never was a Chester Drums. He was a character made up for a short story I wrote back in the twenties. My head is filled with fictional characters I've created over the years. It's not like you can shut them out. It's as if they really do exist. Sometimes I forget who's real and who's not."

Shelly was surprised, but at least he was honest.

"Trust me, I'm not a lunatic," he continued, "I'm just way too involved with my own mind."

"Tell me about old age," she said, quietly proud that she could be so bold.

John did not even hesitate.

"It's weird," he said, "but when I was a kid I always had this picture of a wise old man surrounded by loving grandchildren, as if growing old was always smooth and slow, as if comfort and knowledge were the total package. Not quite. Your body hurts, your eyes blur, your mind battles confusion, hearing is difficult, naps are essential, you can't open the damn medicine bottles, and there goes the weekend.

"And, maybe worst of all, nobody wants to look at you. It's as if they're approaching a graveyard. You're old, you're slow, you're boring, you're dead. They don't want to be reminded of that. They're young, they're alive, so they yank their eyes away." John's expression tightened.

"It's hard to accept being ignored," he said, "like you don't exist, like you really don't matter at all."

"But you don't necessarily grow old inside?" asked Shelly, wondering if that was the best way to phrase the question. "I mean, your mind stays young, doesn't it?"

"Sometimes," he said. "On the best of days, I don't even realize I'm old. I'll think, almost believe, that I'm still moving as a young man, that my face is still the same as it was in 1928. I'm usually a bit shocked when I look into a mirror. What the hell happened? This can't be me. Where'd I go?

"Old people are like ugly children. Go to bed early and stay off the dance floor."

\* \* \* \*

There was more to the interview. For some reason, John felt strong around this girl. She seemed to ignite an almost sensual intensity, an intellect that he often tried to hide or simply had forgotten he even possessed.

He spoke of being young.

"It was another world, another life, now long lost," he said. "There are strands of thoughts and feelings that, every now and then, return for a moment to take me back. But it's never complete, never satisfying.

"And, you know, it's curious that my being born very late in 1899 might somehow be a big deal to anyone at all. Birth carries no choices regarding time. Hemingway was still a kid when I was born and Steinbeck would not write *Grapes of Wrath* for another thirty years. That my birth fell on this precise date on the calendar was total coincidence. Hardly mysterious, it was but my moment to enter life. Obviously, if I now had a decision in the matter, I would have deferred my entrance until 1979. That would make me 20 years old. A perfect age, don't you think?"

"What do you remember about being 20?" Shelly asked.

"When I was 20, my friends were 20, the world was 20. And being that age was not something I even thought about or appreciated. Oh, I'd love to rearrange time."

John also talked about the one woman he had truly loved. He spoke quietly of the child they had buried.

"It was 1950, like a hammer to the soul," he whispered. "Sarah was left only to my dreams and I would awaken cold, sweating, and angry. She was so close, yet never really there. My beautiful child. It was all so very impossible."

John looked at his hands, but continued talking.

"It was the same when I was awake. I thought about her constantly; strained to see her face, hear what I thought might be her voice, capture her smell for just another instant. All I wanted was just a touch of her. Just a touch, to somehow pull her back. It was as if the pain had become more real than Sarah herself.

"Like a billion people before me, I grieved alone. At first it was every day, every hour, every moment. But, eventually, memory began to retreat ever so slightly, just like they always say it will. It was almost a relief, in some ways. It was as if I carried some sort of devastating disease; to love your daughter with so much of your soul.

"And then it seemed to almost disappear—the sounds, the smell, the feel. There became a time that an entire day went past and I didn't even think of her. Later on, it might be a few days, then a few weeks, then only once in a while. Just a passing image I would often try to ignore."

John stopped, as if momentarily searching for his little girl.

"God, 50 years later, it's still so hard to talk about," he said, trying to push his words past choking tears. "Lately, she's returned to my dreams, all the time. I can feel her at the edge of my shadow, a sad comfort."

He stopped again. Shelly wondered if she should change the subject. Let him talk, she thought.

And he did.

"Strange, but in my dreams, she never lives with me. She always arrives from somewhere else. Or I go pick her up, then have to take her back. She's very quiet, very lonesome. I can tell."

\* \* \* \*

Shelly found herself drifting inside an emotion of painted pictures, both haunting and beautiful.

Floored by an old man's stories.

The interview went much longer than she had planned. Surely John must be tired, but she was the one who felt drained. There was so much more to this man that she now felt cheated the filming had to end.

Well, the plan was for one short interview, not returning until the actual birthday party on New Year's Eve. Even that had seemed an inconvenience at first. Was this the way she wanted to usher in the new century? What if she had a date?

Now, it didn't matter. She quickly realized that this study of an old man was much deeper than she had initially assumed. This was more than a short film to pass along for Daniel Stroud's video scrapbook.

"This has been so very interesting," she said, a strong trace of affection in her voice. "But I just realized we never really talked about your days as a sportswriter. I wonder if I could come back?"

He didn't even pause.

"That would be great," he said, wondering if his response might seem too anxious.

"Would Monday morning about 11 be okay?" she asked.

"No problem," he said.

Two days, he thought, two long days.

She smiled and their eyes locked for just an instant. Whoa, if he could just hold onto that moment.

"Thanks for the interview," she said.

Business.

This was just business.

\* \* \* \*

John was tired, his nerves racing, his body beaten. He moved slowly into his chair, but his head felt extremely light. The trance struck quickly.

The cliff.

He tried to shake it out of his mind, but couldn't. Not the cliff, not again.

And once more he saw the plunge, felt his stomach churn in panic as air refused to cushion the desperate fall.

John tried to blink, tried to pull away, but once again he was trapped inside his little girl's flight.

No escape.

# CHAPTER 5

That night, Shelly sat in her makeshift office, pretending she was something she obviously wasn't. A few walls away, her parents silently watched television, their world secure.

Shelly realized her problems—far too much reliance on those who loved her, a fear of standing alone and taking chances, a career in slow motion.

With the life of John Hammond consuming her thoughts, she charted two scenarios—one was fame, the other a frustrating and bitter failure. She had to work, she had to move. Struggle had to be embraced.

Demanding that her mind embrace effort, she diligently observed her day's work on film, moving closer to the monitor, staring at the face of a 99-year-old man. Listening to John's string of memories, the dilemma of her lethargic career completely vanished into a flow of rejuvenated energy.

Shelley chuckled at her initial reluctance to take this project, her mind now pushing to possibilities far beyond what Daniel Stroud had requested.

John Hammond was fascinating; all he had seen, all he had done, all he was, and all he wasn't.

John never did say how his child had died. She had wanted to ask, but didn't. But this was something she needed to know. Great reporters have no problem asking difficult questions.

Just as Daniel Stroud had warned, John showed an obvious uneasiness concerning his family. He seemed guarded, eager to change the subject.

And here was the part about World War I where he was talking about the death of Chester Drums, still standing with a bullet in his face? Mr. Hammond had been as convincing as a veteran actor. Shelly wondered if more of his recollections might be fabricated. At his age, John's lines of reality could have strayed to countless directions. For all she knew, a good percentage of old people might tend to exaggerate. Still, the rest of his stories just might be total fact.

Whatever proved true, she loved the wild, creative path he opened within her mind. Yes, her every instinct was to trust him.

But not be like him.

If nothing else, the interview was a powerful lesson about what not to do with brilliance. Unlike John, Shelly would need to manage her creativity. Grabbing a sheet of paper, she jotted a note with large bold letters, "Creative Organized Thinking." Now there was a concept to stamp across her forehead.

Spotlighting the smaller details of the day's filming, Shelly began to concentrate less on John's words and more on his eyes. She would expect such ancient eyes to be clouded and distant, but John's seemed almost vibrant. The surrounding walls were red and crumbling, but the eyes themselves seemed to scorn the imprisonment.

They had a passion, she thought, like a rebel on a sacred journey. All around are the scars of disaster; but his eyes are still deep in battle, one last bastion of youth.

On the other hand, perhaps she was just getting carried away by her own crazed imagination. Maybe the eyes were as frail as the body. Even a dying antelope, its neck twisted inside the jaws of an unknown predator, keeps its eyes wide open, no doubt in shock, no doubt in fear.

And some might suggest that a tight camera on an old man, his face filling the screen, might agitate the viewer. Too old, too vulgar, too close to death—change the channel.

As John had mentioned during the filming, the young really don't want to deal with the old. Nobody wants to think about dying. So the beautiful people look away, distracted by wrinkle-free skin. As for the elders, they apparently learn to accept being ignored. It's all very cultural, thought Shelly, very foolish.

But also very true. She herself was constantly guilty of the snub, as if old people were somehow less. How could she break that down on film?

Because if you look at John Hammond just a little deeper, you will see something entirely different than decimated age. There is a beauty to these lines, Shelly reasoned. They are shaped by thousands of unique moments, the work of an artist forever locked in an unfinished masterpiece.

Shelly paused. John had her thinking the way he talked. Something had sprung in her brain, dribbling out a pool or poetic words.

"Creative Organized Thinking," she repeated aloud, signaling the live conversation she was about to hold with herself.

"In fact, moving still closer into the lines of age could capture the viewer," she said as her mind rushed with possibilities.

"That's it," she said. "The camera needs to be even closer to his face. The old man will draw in the viewers, offering no escape for what we all must become."

So simple, yet so bold. This could work. This could be riveting. This could be her chance.

Yep, she was thinking just like John.

\* \* \* \*

In Escondido, John Hammond was processing the interview. He had remembered that his attention had been focused on Shelly's lips. They were full, giving her face a very unique and sensuous look, at least to him.

Geez, she's a young girl, he quickly told his disobedient mind.

But her mouth was quite alluring; and he felt a certain sense of pride that he could still notice these things, particularly in light of the belief that old men eventually lose their sexual appetites. What kind of nonsense was that?

And there was something else about the interview; an uneasy feeling, as if he had not been honest. But at this moment, he couldn't remember exactly what was even said.

\* \* \* \*

Shelly's adrenaline was cruising at warp speed.

This was not the herky-jerky, shake-the-lens, "let's play idiot for the camera" routine that had been so ridiculously popular since the early '90s. To her senses, that method of filming was simply inserting flash-and-noise to hide a lack of creativity.

Shelly was not interested in being trite. Her art was not a joke. This was good stuff.

And best of all, perhaps for the first time, Shelly felt as if she was on the verge of becoming a true filmmaker.

"Don't blow it," she whispered to herself.

\* \* \* \*

John was attempting to picture himself when he was Shelly's age. That would have been somewhere around 1928.

In fact, that was the year he had taken a summer trip from Pennsylvania to California, most of the journey on the new Route 66. He was alone with his golden lab, Rapture, the best dog he ever loved. They cruised "The Main Street of America" heading west in a brand new 1927 Chrysler "72" Roadster with a rumble seat. They called it the "72" because Walter Chrysler guaranteed his automobile could go at least that fast. Chrysler also sold an Imperial "80" that really hauled.

John recalled hitting 60 miles an hour for a short stretch somewhere past Joplin but feared his black "72" might break down if he pushed too hard. His father had loaned him $1,500 to buy the car. Once again realizing he had never repaid the old man, John's mind tightened and closed, promptly erasing the debt for the thousandth time.

The summer of 1928. There was a girl, beautiful and much younger than him. It came back to him now; she had just turned 21.

They had met at Lake Arrowhead, both traveling and camping. She lived in Laguna Beach, he remembered, and had been spending her vacation drawing trees and writing. They were much alike.

What was her name? He could see her dark hair, piercing blue eyes and skin he had to touch. They spent an entire day kissing and holding and falling deeply in love. And that night, alone in her cabin, they became intimate. She was beautiful. It seemed so very real and natural.

John twitched. For some odd reason, a stray thought of failure began growing in his mind; an irritation at first, just festering, soon taking command of his entire being. This couldn't be, but it was.

And now John remembered. She had been passionate, while he busily questioned his manhood. What was wrong? Where was his strength, his power?

He had pulled away, made up some excuse about his mind getting in the way, apologized, and left; too ashamed to even stay an extra second, to maybe take a deep breath, to maybe talk, to maybe hold each other. No, he had already gone.

He had known for years that he had been unbearably unkind, that she didn't deserve such foolish and insensitive behavior.

But, at the time, he just wanted to escape.

He never saw her again.

With Rapture riding shotgun in the Chrysler Roadster, they headed for Big Bear, then down the mountain to Redlands. The land itself was spectacular, mile upon mile of orange groves in a valley that seemed to ride the San Bernardino Mountains all the way to Los Angeles and the Pacific Ocean, the panorama of a lifetime.

That was the moment that John could easily have turned around, drove back to Lake Arrowhead, or even searched for her home in Laguna Beach. But that would mean he would need to admit fault, to ask forgiveness, to crawl. It was not in his nature.

Instead, after a week or so in San Clemente and San Diego, he headed east to Yuma, then up to Phoenix and Flagstaff, further and further away. He often thought of her, regretting his callousness and shame. Maybe if he had just gone back, life would have taken a different path, a better path, or not.

Now, she'd be almost 93, perhaps waiting for him in a cozy rest home on the California coastline, a couple of hours from Escondido, never losing hope that he would return. Despite a broken heart, she had probably aged quite well.

Or she had traveled to another part of the world, married a man of unknown qualities, had children, grandchildren, great grandchildren. Maybe, every so often, she thought about John and what might have been.

No, she was probably dead.

It would be nice if he could remember her name.

* * * *

John was curled under his blanket, hoping to recall the feeling of strength, long breaths and tight muscles; to run, to jump from rock to rock, to walk without pain. Now, it was nothing more than a remote shadow.

But now he noticed that his right arm was beginning to feel quite numb. Just ignore it, he told himself.

Just relax . . .

One of John's most profound realizations over the years was that aches and pains did not always signal death. If he could just relax his mind, the pain would diminish. It had taken years, but he had finally conditioned his brain to a certain ignorance of death, like an animal without the ability to process reason or thought. Or a young child without the knowledge that life will someday end; because, to a child's mind, for life to stop is simply impossible to fathom, until that first jolt of unwanted information is repeated again and again.

The first attack to John's brain must have occurred around the age of four; a boy barely delving into rationality and logic, still residing at the center of the universe. What, he wondered, was underneath those gravestones next to the church? People stuck in the ground forever, his distressed mind had calculated. How could they breathe? How could they move? How could they think?

But certainly those dead people in their graves had nothing to do with Johnny Hammond. He would live forever, wouldn't he?

Ever so slowly, he realized he wouldn't. Now, of course, there was no doubt, what with his body falling apart.

The fear of death could strike at any time, so it was best not to consider it at all, not to ponder the eternal nothingness. Except sometimes he would be caught off guard, the shock that this would be his final moment of life always horrifying. Always.

Finally, John's arm had feeling. No need to panic. Close, but he would live. He just needed to rest.

\* \* \* \*

John was aware it was a dream and, for some strange reason, felt excited, as if he was going on another long and exciting adventure, perhaps a vacation.

He had a vague notion that he was awake, but certainly he must be asleep because he felt extremely strong. Still, it was not often that he could reason during a dream, so perhaps he wasn't asleep, just locked in a trance.

No, he was dreaming, because he now realized the walls were distant and hollow, and he was young.

John immediately noticed that he was in a newsroom, but it was much different than he remembered. The room was packed with reporters and editors who were obviously busy. John was at his desk. Pete Castle, his old sports editor, approached from behind.

"Deadline's in 10 minutes," he said. "Where's your story?"

Story? What story?

John began to panic. He had never missed a deadline, but he had no idea what his story was even supposed to be about. There was no way he could finish. He needed more time. How'd he get into this jam?

"Five minutes to deadline," yelled Pete. "Where's your story?"

John suddenly realized that everything was now done by computer. Writing, editing and page layout would be much faster. Yes, that would be the answer; he'd just use the computer. Except he didn't know the codes. He didn't even know the password to log into the damn computer. Failure was certain.

"One minute to deadline," boomed Pete. "We need everything now."

Stress belted John from his restless sleep, his body startled, his thoughts uncertain . . .

John's mind was slow and hazy, but it was good to be awake and even better that the newsroom was gone.

It was weird, John would later realize, but he had experienced a number of similar dreams. The newsroom changed, but the underlying plot was always the same; deadline fast approaching and he was totally unprepared.

\* \* \* \*

Late into the night, Shelly finally turned off the video. She had devised a solid plan. She needed to work the light, get the camera in close for detail. The viewer would have no retreat. This story was simply too fascinating.

The problem would be selling the concept. Hey everyone, rush to your local theater so you can see this blockbuster documentary about an old man getting ready to die.

Plus, there were holes.

She needed the storyline to be deeper, the questions to be sharper. She needed to somehow get inside his mind, to show his heart and soul, strengths and fears.

She could attack it historically. After all, he had said he was a different person every five years of his life. She could start at the beginning and chronologically unwind this marvelous tale.

No, she thought, that's been done a thousand times. True film-makers don't repeat stale formulas.

Perhaps she should just let him drift along with his stories, then edit the film to artistically create the true character of the man. She could splice the boredom to leave him exciting and bold, mysterious and wise, quick and humorous.

With hard work and magic, she could almost make him handsome, provided she could lure the viewer past the wrinkles and into his eyes. That would be key; to fire his flaws so close to the viewer that they would be seen as scars of beauty.

But what if the old man does not cooperate? What if Monday he changes his attitude and doesn't want to talk? What if his mind finally snaps and all he can do is babble?

She realized there were potential problems.

\* \* \* \*

By the next day, John had solved his problem.

Bottom line, it was a passing case of foolishness. Young girls don't fall in love with old men, so it was not a matter that could ever be pursued.

He had to be realistic. He had to ignore stray emotions, no matter how powerful.

Sure, the girl may have ignited some long-dormant spark inside his body, or perhaps it was just a side effect of his many medicines, a bad dose that just happened to kick in when he first saw her. It was just coincidence, just a mistake.

After all, maturity arrives with boundaries and limitations. There are rules to being old and one of the most obvious is that you don't crash deeply in love with someone three or four generations removed. It doesn't work, ever, and that is understood.

Five or ten years, no problem. Twenty years, pushing the limit. Thirty years, warped. As for a seven-decade age difference? Well, that would be absurd, beyond ridiculous, and should no longer be considered.

Besides, all of this would only matter provided she even loved him, which she didn't. Any hint of attraction he even imagined she might have sent his way was no more than everyday kindness.

John rubbed his forehead.

Maybe in another time, another universe; but not here, not in this age, not on this planet, where most people fall in love and marry within their own school grade. She's 15 years old and he's been dead for two centuries, a perfect couple should they ever decide to link their souls rather than follow the cultural norms of automatic attraction according to birth dates.

Plus, even if he did want to profess this love, there was no one he could tell, particularly Shelly.

"I'm in love with the most beautiful person in the world," he could proclaim, "and she's only 72 years younger than me."

That would be slick.

But, yes, he did love her; totally, beyond doubt, with a passion he could never reveal. He just had to hold it inside as an impossible truth. For the most part, he had to realize it was yet another sign he was teetering on the brink of a final collapse.

He needed to record some of these thoughts. Where did he put that notebook?

Inspired by the moment, John quickly started scribbling.

*Few people grow old with dignity anymore. They become too engulfed in what they aren't and will never be again. They become obsessed, senseless.*

*Eventually they are like quiet shadows, listening to the sound of each breath. They sit and stare, always cautious. Don't move, don't die.*

*But, somewhere, in the far corner of the brain, one stray electron keeps blasting the Rock 'n Roll, trying desperately to rekindle passions that retreated when the skin began to wither and the body no longer cared.*

*The old were once so quick, so strong. Now they're just confused, obscure.*

*It's the mind that won't let go . . .*

That's totally true, he thought, grabbing a different sheet of paper.

*I must eliminate this absurd notion from my brain. I can never really love Shelly and she certainly will never fall in love with me. In fact, this isn't love at all; just some crazy strain of lust.*

*And, even if, for some unbelievable reason, Shelly did love me, how could it possibly last?*

*Making love with her would need to be more than just a lucky moment. It would require continual strength. I would need to establish a pace, keep it exciting and stimulating, perhaps even erotic.*

*Oops, I am completely whacked out of my mind.*

John reread the four paragraphs, pushed his rolling chair away from the desk, painfully crossed the room and deposited the "love sheet" into the new shredder Daniel had bought for him.

"Don't need no evidence," John whispered as the blades chomped.

Still, he refused to back down.

There was another important consideration, he realized. How quickly would the routine turn stale?

At first, she probably wouldn't even expect him to perform sexually, but he'd get carried away and try to move like a 40-year-old. He'd kill himself.

It would be best just to hold her. That would be enough; even though he needed more, as did she.

Stop pretending, John told himself. How could any love break through such impossible obstacles? It couldn't.

Just knock it off. Stop thinking of fascinating possibilities that will never happen. It's not worth the agony.

\* \* \* \*

There, it was settled. There would be no hunt, no candlelight dinners, no all-night dancing, no love. All it took was a strong dose of reality.

He felt better, he felt alone.

# CHAPTER 6

Sunday evening, the walk was slow. Smog and filth had been pounded down by rain, so the sky was particularly clear. Already John could see Mars nestled close to the moon's sliver, a point toward infinity, trillions of stars and galaxies stretching forever.

Life beyond the solar cloak? Death simply the doorway to another dimension? Will the soul be allowed to see, to hear, to touch? He should shut these thoughts out. Questions of religion and physics always seem to lead to conclusions of nothingness. No existence, no soul, no thoughts, no hope.

John's body began to quiver. Leave it alone, he thought. Don't fall into this nonsense. Think of other things. Think about baseball, movies, dogs, beautiful women.

But his brain refused such petty distractions.

If death is forever nothing, he told himself, then none of this really matters, because life is not recalled. It is an eternal instant, forever unknown.

Then again, if infinity travels outward, it must also travel inward. Forever must flow in endless directions. Perhaps the soul resides in the infinite depths of the mind or heart. Perhaps death is but an inward journey. Perhaps there is hope.

*Death would be but a lost moment never to be recovered . . . and it would not hurt.*

And every so often, John became almost relaxed about his impending death, as if finally he would know the ultimate truth.

Perhaps his mind, even his body, would transfer to another realm on the far side of some distant universe. Or maybe his soul, if there really is such a thing, would reunite with the souls of those he had known. Having lost his trust in the Sunday School version of life, he had long been pounded by the endless possibilities.

The important thing in death, he reasoned, is just to feel something, to somehow be able to think, to once again hold the people he has loved.

But comforting theories of eternal life seldom last. Eventually, John drove himself back to a frightening state of fear. Wrapped in near panic, he would realize that most likely death is nothing but a void, an eternal blank that erases all that ever was and all that ever will be again.

*Time winds down, percentages dwindle, another life span reaches its conclusion. Nothing survives . . . absolutely nothing.*

These were the thoughts John jotted into his latest notebook. The night before, he had been working on ideas for a story about a man turning 40 who had never made love, had never even come close to being intimate. John had started this book a number of years ago, originally a touching piece of quiet desperation. But the more John got into the story, the more the central character pissed him off. This guy wasn't shy, he was weak.

Certainly, John was caring and sensitive. Women were to be respected. Even when the concept wasn't all that fashionable, John had realized that women were being abused by society in general, idiotic men in particular. He had always understood that women were victims of cultural quirks that were unfair, biased and absurd.

At the same time, it seemed to John that man's natural drive was to have them, to feast upon their bodies, to love them with both power and passion, to leave them wanting more.

Anything less was reserved for wimps.

And, no matter how enlightened a man might be regarding gender equity, the art of man conquering woman was still a primal truth, or at least an urge.

Or so he remembered.

Maybe that wasn't quite accurate, he told himself as if this were an intimate conversation being broadcast to 85 million people on a special edition of *60 Minutes*. There was, after all, a passionate sharing between lovers, two coming together as one. Certainly, the basis of love is equality. Perhaps *conquering* was too strong of a word to describe man's sexual drive towards woman.

He had a few more notes on the subject, but they were displaced at the moment. Well, anyway, it wasn't that great of a story.

Forget the whole thing, he muttered to himself. It would only get him into trouble.

* * * *

To hell with thoughts of death and men who can't get laid. John needed to lighten up, perhaps insert some humor back into his writings.

His writings? Who was he kidding? His life's production was nothing more than bundles of meaningless notes, volumes of unfinished hopes, far too scattered with no time to get it right.

He must admit failure. He would never finish anything.

\* \* \* \*

The same could probably be said for *The Brave Historian.* Robert Patterson was also a man of no direction or conclusion.

And John was growing tired of his company. Robert Patterson desperately needed an adventure, a purpose beyond what had become nothing more than a boring existence. The man needed to be bold.

Then again, thought John, the guy isn't even real.

\* \* \* \*

John slowly opened the kitchen door. His hands hurt. Why were knobs so hard to maneuver?

Daniel was sitting at the table, working on bills.

"Hey," Daniel said, barely looking up. "Did you have a good walk?"

"It was okay," said John. "Not as cold as yesterday."

"Radio said we might get into the high 70s by mid-week," said Daniel. "That's great for December."

"Well, February always seems to be the coldest around here," said John, further lengthening another conversation without substance.

"Must have been cold growing up in Pennsylvania," Daniel mumbled.

"It was a different kind of cold," said John. "I loved the seasons."

Daniel said nothing in return, his mind escaping back to his chart of payments.

John kept walking, heading for the safety of another room.

\* \* \* \*

Daniel could feel the anger preparing to strike. This was ridiculous. Life had become a journey to someday break even. He worked too damn hard.

"Always broke," he grumbled at the table, wondering how regular people could afford to live.

He should team with a famous economist and write a best-seller about the financial decline of the middle class. Then, he too would be rich.

As for now, the Stroud family's economic forecast was pathetic.

Plus, having yet another person in the house was even more draining. His wife had warned him.

"It's a ridiculous idea," she said bluntly. "We can't afford to have John live here, even if he is a good friend of yours. How are we supposed to take care of him?"

But Daniel was convinced this would be a wise gesture.

"It will only be for a few months," he promised. "I really want to collaborate on this book idea we've been kicking around. I mean, this will give us the time and space to finally get it finished. And in the long run it could bring us a lot of money."

"You can't count on money that's not there yet," said Katherine.

Daniel gave himself pause as he prepared for the "sensitivity" argument, one Katherine never believed.

"He was my grandfather's best friend," said Daniel.

"I know, Daniel," interrupted Katherine. "You've known him

all your life. He came to your baseball games when you were a boy, never missed a birthday, helped you through college. He's like family to you. I get it. But that doesn't mean we need to take care of him."

"I just don't want him to spend his 100th birthday in a nursing home," he exclaimed, again. "It wouldn't be fair."

"There are thousands of people turning 100 in rest homes," Katherine replied. "It's where they live. You need to go to his home and work on your books at a corner table."

"No, you don't understand," said Daniel. "We have way too many notes and boxes. There's no way we could be organized. We need a private space."

"It's just such a heavy commitment," she said.

"He won't be any trouble and he can sleep in the guest room," said Daniel. "This will be a lot easier than you think. The kids love him and he's so quiet you'll hardly even notice he's here. Besides, how much longer does he have to live?"

"I don't know," said Katherine, "how about another 20 years. He might outlive both of us. You don't know when a person is going to drop over and die. And did it ever occur to you that he might develop some drastic health issue that could suddenly consume our lives. We have to be reasonable. I think John living here could turn into a major problem."

"We'll put a deadline on it," said Daniel. "I'll explain to him it will only be until early June. I'll tell him we're going back east when school ends. I'll tell him we're planning a long vacation, so that would be the time we would have to take him back to Pepper Tree. I'll tell him that. Plus, he might not even want to live here."

But he did. John didn't even hesitate when asked. The chance for change was too alluring.

"Great idea," he had said, not even considering this might

be an inconvenience to Daniel's family. No, this was an escape from the old folk's home, from the constant reminder of misery. Now there would be laughter and kids and family. Now he could play his old piano again. He was already feeling younger.

A smile blazed across John's face as he suddenly pictured the sign taped above that assembly-line piano at Pepper Tree Retirement Prison: *No Piano Playing Past 9:00 p.m.—Absolutely No Exceptions.*

No more of that nonsense. He was back in the game.

\* \* \* \*

This was an invitation that should only be viewed as a kind and noble gesture. And, yes, Daniel deeply cared for John. Still, there was another reason Daniel had asked John to spend the winter with them, one that nagged at John's ethical balance— the payoff when the old man died.

Back in 1988, when John sold his home and moved to Pepper Tree Retirement Village, he had asked Daniel to store some of his possessions. John's piano, which he had owned for nearly 70 years, sat in the corner of the living room where different members of the family could bang on it from time to time. Other treasures included three paintings by Mary Hammond, a packet of David Hammond's hand-written notes, and several family scrapbooks packed with pictures and articles dating back to the turn of the century. In a world of memorabilia-gone-mad, Daniel realized the value of actual Hammond items just might be beyond belief.

Even more, the entire loft in Daniel's back garage housed about 40 cardboard boxes belonging to John. These contained old magazines, books, personal remembrances, even a few baseball cards. A lot of it was just an old man's collection of junk, but some of it could be worth a good bit of money.

Perhaps the best cache might be found in the dozen or so boxes filled with John's writings—manuscripts, notes, diaries, poems and music.

True, John had never really invited Daniel to study any of his private writings. That Daniel spent hours hunched in the attic of his garage reading the old man's stray words was a secret, never discussed. And it was not that Daniel was a snoop. No, he was a teacher. Curiosity was his drive, his craving, his license. Of course, the words could someday be worth millions.

It was John's diaries that initially struck Daniel's attention.

> *October 14, 1918: Heading for war. How could that be? Right this minute, I should be sitting in class at Bucknell, not sailing across the Atlantic. But it turns out that a C-average isn't acceptable to my father and he bullies me into joining the Army. He says it's time for me to grow up, but that's not the real issue. He's got some battle hymn he's pushing and how would it look if America's most patriotic bandmaster tried to shelter his oldest son from the far shores of Europe? The worst part is that I'm scared and not sure how to hide it.*

The diaries were scattered into a number of notebooks with apparently no regard for organization.

> *August 5, 1937: David sent a letter saying he's written a book that's going to be published. He's calling it "Blue Gold" and I have no idea what it possibly could be about. Funny, because all this time I thought he was just freeloading off father. Now it turns out he's an author.*

*March 20, 1949: Father's health is failing. His face seems so pale, his skin like a blue and pasty chalk. He'll sit at the piano for hours and only play "Soft Return." But he does love to be with Sarah. Though I can tell he's near death, my little girl seems to give him a reason to live.*

There were years and years of stuff. It struck Daniel that he could write a history of the 20th century based solely upon the old man's experiences and observations.

Of course, it wasn't like these were the private diaries of Franklin Roosevelt or Adolf Hitler or even Wilt "The Stilt" Chamberlain. But, how many people had lived through an entire century and bothered to take notes? Surely, this was an historical coup. Daniel had been stuck in slow gear for too long. To someday edit these works would surely be his great break in life, a chance to finally leap from mediocrity.

One other thing. While Daniel considered himself a student of precise diction, he was nevertheless enthralled by the old man's rather imaginative fiction, a path that veered far from reality. It was definitely different from the literature Daniel assigned his high school students to read.

He particularly liked a piece from a manuscript John had titled *The Last Living Child of India*, the entire story occurring within one man's mind.

*It had been a quiet and peaceful walk until he turned against the wind. He had not felt it at his back, but now its force pestered his movement, crackled loud against his ears.*

*And then it stopped, for no apparent reason. There was a hint of warmth, but the sun was too*

*far south to break the chill. The momentary silence
was broken by distant crows feasting on a bloated
carcass, chattering loudly amongst themselves,
prepared to take flight at the slightest disturbance.*

*He sensed the ravens viewed him with disdain. No
pity, no heart, they just continued to dine.*

Daniel would sometimes read a sentence or paragraph several times, as if he were unraveling a puzzle complete with hidden meanings. The opening lines of *Pirate Ships*, for example, roamed the walls of his mind like a song he could not shake.

*In all things considered, it was the wrong direction.
Still why should he set his course to the north, where
the pale ice swallows the sea?*

\* \* \* \*

*The Man with Total Control* had Daniel both intrigued and baffled. For one, unlike John's other works, this rather short novel seemed to be finished. There was no hint as to when it might have been written, but Daniel was surprised and angry it had never been published. Who wouldn't want to read such an amazing story? Except, of course, it was strange.

He had read the book three times. Each reading seemed to produce different meanings, unconventional paradoxes to yank at his mind.

It both troubled and fascinated Daniel how much he associated with the story's main character, Jeremy Mueller. It was something Daniel would admit only to himself, but he also felt "trapped within these walls," a prisoner of his own private universe.

*Sitting down with the pen, forcing himself to create, the poet searches for brilliance. But, alas, he is afraid of mistakes and the paper remains blank.*

*"Wait," he tells himself. "I am much better than this foolishness. My mind must know more than I am thinking."*

*Finally, the pen moves and the fingers follow. But the words are confusing, the lines jagged, stale verse shattering his ego.*

*"What I am loses to what I am not," he scribbles. "God hides the perversions He loves."*

Quite frankly, Daniel wasn't exactly sure if some of this stuff was genius or trash. He just knew that despite the strange nature of John's fictional works, they were sure fun to read. He liked the mystery, the intrigue, the uneasiness they created. He liked riding into someone else's peculiar mind, as if it had somehow become his own.

*We exist on a cliff and suddenly I am sliding in mud. I stretch for a final rock, but miss and fall away from what once was. My only hope is a miracle, for one hand to grab me and hold me for just another moment.*

*"We do not need you," the mob screams as I fall.*

*And now the world has become very historical, very dense, very quiet. It seems that all before me is not there and all behind me is gone.*

*I wake in silence, my mind streaking across the floor, my body defeated. Lost at the edge of panic, I try desperately to hold just one more moment. But, as always, it proves to be impossible.*

# THE BRAVE HISTORIAN

*Down below the noise, I merely sought warmth.*

Daniel reminded himself that the writing did not really fit the personality. John Hammond was not a dark and somber person. He had a wonderful sense of humor. And, despite the handicap of his age, he was always interesting and even fun. Still, his writings seemed to dwell in shadows and obscurity, forever at war with possibilities beyond death. Daniel realized that it must be a long and private battle John kept only to himself and the silence of his words.

> *Predictions grow rampant. I am not without theories and conclusions regarding the possibilities that creation will repeat itself. Unfortunately, the most obvious is the most horrifying; no feeling, no understanding, nothing, not even darkness. I am infinitely nonexistent and thus never known.*
> *I do not fear death . . . I fear nothingness.*

It was more than an intellectual fever that stirred inside the high school English teacher. Don't deny it, this was a discovery. He could edit these works and turn them into prize literature. John Hammond would be remembered as perhaps the greatest writer of his time. And, yes, Daniel Stroud would make a fortune.

Daniel just needed something like a contract to assure that he would inherit John's writings and avoid any possible legal problems. It was good John had no living relatives. Daniel's claim to these boxes would be for the sake of history and literature.

So, he wasn't being totally deceptive.

Except Daniel didn't really want the old man living at his home. Daniel understood that such thoughts were selfish and wrong. He tried to ignore the twinge of guilt he now battled.

Welcome to my home and give me your life's work. That's enough, old man, you're intruding into my space.

* * * *

It had been several years earlier that Daniel had made the suggestion that the two collaborate. John always had a pad and pen, forever jotting down thoughts and observations. While he had shared none of them with Daniel, the two of them had spent much time discussing the art of writing. John had even lectured several of Daniel's high school English classes on the subject.

Although Daniel never revealed his private intrusions into John's writings, he did offer encouragement to the old man.

"Why don't you publish some of the things you write about?" he had asked.

"Oh, I don't know," said John. "I've never really tried. And I think it's a bit late now."

"It's never too late, John. You should know that."

"Well, I do have plenty of material. I guess I've just been waiting for the right moment. You know, for the president of a great publishing house to bust through my door."

"Well, maybe you need to go to them."

"That's undoubtedly true," said John, "but I really wouldn't know where to begin. Besides, I just like to imagine ideas and stories and write them down. There's not that much I have really completed. And, most of all, I don't need any rejections at this stage of my life."

"Well, maybe all you need is a little push in the right direction," said Daniel. "Maybe I could help you edit something. We could get it finished, then send it off to some agents and publishers. Put the ball in their court. Who knows what might happen?"

The old man smiled.

"That would be nice," he said. "I suppose it's worth a try. There is one book I'd like to wrap up. It's called *The Brave Historian*. I'm not quite sure what direction it's going, but if you do want to try your hand at editing and perhaps even cheerleading, I think we'd make a great team. Hey, a new blast of energy might be good for me."

So, with that small beginning, John and Daniel shook hands and set out to complete a prize novel. Good intentions, little time.

They started strong. For a while, they met every Saturday morning for two hours. The plan was to discuss thoughts and style. At John's insistence, they would view themselves as artists—never copying, always creating. At Daniel's insistence, they would push for a completed manuscript.

Daniel quickly discovered that editing John's work would be a challenge. Grammatically, he was near perfect. The copy was clean, the words meaningful. The problem, to Daniel, was the intensity.

"Too intense," said Daniel. "Your reader has to be too intelligent, too focused."

"Good," said John, "because most surveys conclude that stupid people don't read."

"It's just that some of this stuff is so complex," said Daniel, "that I am afraid the reader is being pulled inside the writer's thoughts one moment, then shut out the next."

"But that's the way life is," said John.

"Maybe so," replied Daniel, "but it's not the way literature necessarily works."

"Daniel, it's too late for lessons on compound sentences and comma splices," mused John. "I don't want to fit inside that square. At this point, I could care less."

"I just think that sometimes it needs a little more order," said Daniel.

Order was probably not the best word, but Daniel was sold that he needed to play a stronger role as editor. For one thing, he believed *The Brave Historian* should be chronological. After all, it was about a teacher of 20th century history. And although Robert Patterson was fictional, the book did include a number of historical anecdotes.

"Why would I want it to be by day or year?" John argued. "It's not about history. It's about a guy who studies history and his assumption of its importance until he realizes he's locked in the library, that he's lost the sun. And, by the way, he eventually recognizes the truth that the past really doesn't matter all that much. We don't learn from history. We throw it away. It's over, it's gone, it does not exist. Nothing stops for the past."

That was as much of a story outline as Daniel ever received from John.

"Is it possible," argued John, "that every plot in the world has already been done? I really don't want to purchase Rapid Writer's Plot Outline #173 from the Sears Catalogue and then add a bunch of sentences. We are exploring, my boy, and when our manuscript is done, it will be unique, and then everybody else will copy us."

"John, this is great stuff," said Daniel. "I just sometimes think you prefer mood over substance. I don't know if the reader can follow some of this."

"They said the same thing about Bob Dylan," laughed John. "And probably anyone else who's ever been unusual. The reader is supposed to be getting into the writer's head, not the other way around."

Daniel realized the editing would be a lot easier if John were already dead. As for now, it wasn't working.

\* \* \* \*

John had a different take on the partnership.

He had always done his best writing late at night, when the world was quiet and his mind most alert. He was creative, reckless; but hated the fatigue that always followed the next day. And he was too damn old to easily bounce back.

It would be best to write in the morning. It would be best to write alone.

Daniel understood John's creative needs, but also felt the need to push, to be the perfect editor.

And so they wrote and talked and pondered, adept at losing time and focus. Daniel was busy at home when he wasn't teaching and John had a tendency to wander into other projects. Their work began to plod.

Both knew they needed a creative spark. Perhaps Shelly Kingston's documentary would light that fire.

\* \* \* \*

John was aware it was a dream. The valley was hollow, the gray sky had no depth.

No problem, he had a baseball game to play and, certainly, he would be the cleanup hitter. Only the guy making the batting order inserted himself at the number four position, and this guy was a wimp.

Still, hitting third or fifth would be satisfactory. John had always prided himself on the fact that he was a team player. Except, now he noticed some other guys would be hitting in those spots. Geez, what's going on?

Seventh? He was hitting in the seven-hole? That's for short-stops and .250 hitters. This was an insult. Sluggers don't bat seventh.

Okay, calm down, doesn't matter. Whatever the order, John would show them just how good he was. Having mastered the art of hitting, he'd give the ball a ride, smack it into the cen-terfield bleachers. The secret was just to see the ball from the pitcher's hand and get the fat part of the bat out in front of the plate, make solid contact, cut the ball in two, rip the hell out of it.

Simple.

And stay loose, deep breath, hands away from the body, don't think, just react.

Standing in the dugout, John studied the opposing pitcher. The guy was nothing special. John would crank it for sure. No doubt the fans would be impressed.

Wait, he was up. Already? What about the on-deck circle? He hadn't even had time to stretch.

"Get up to the plate, hot shot," the umpire grumbled.

Wait a second. Ballplayers just don't walk up there cold. He needed to swing a couple of bats to loosen up. But there was no time.

"You got about two seconds, batter."

"Okay, okay," John mumbled while moving into the batter's box, digging in at the plate.

Confidence, he told himself. Eyes on the ball, mind clear.

But he could not shake the notion that the bat seemed heavy and slightly awkward.

The pitcher began his windup, the ball twisting toward the

plate. John's swing was hard, empty. It wasn't even a good pitch, outside high.

"Strike one," the umpire blurted.

Dumb. But the pitcher was already winding up again. No time to set his feet, figure a plan, build his confidence. Curve, too late, he missed again.

"Strike two," the umpire hollered, as if John's failure brought great joy to his feeble personality.

This was unfair. It was a quick pitch. You can't do that. The ump had to give the hitter at least a couple of seconds to get ready. That was the rule, wasn't it? Of course it was. This was absurd.

John's neck was tight, his arms stiff.

"Miss again and you sit down," the umpire muttered.

Hey, umpires can't say stuff like that. They're supposed to be objective. This guy needed to be reported to somebody. He probably wasn't even a real umpire, probably the pitcher's father. Still, John was a good two-strike hitter, always had been.

No time to think about any of this. John noticed the ball was already in the air and moving toward the plate. It looked big, it looked fat, this was the one.

John's swing was smooth, powerful, pathetic. The pitch was outside low, nearly in the dirt for heaven's sake.

"You're out," bellowed the ump, obviously thrilled.

Go back, that wasn't fair, there were mistakes, he should have another chance.

John awoke, his mind still scorning the near past. He hated failure. Dreams should be line drives and towering homers, he thought, not wild swings at bad pitches in the dirt.

The bat was too heavy.

\* \* \* \*

93

John felt somewhat uneasy that morning, as if a great injustice had occurred, as if he'd been cheated.

"Damn, I should have hit that ball," he said to himself.

And then he stared out the window, the hint of frost beginning to fade, but still no sun, no warmth.

There was another time, of course, when his uniform was stained with dirt and sweat drained freely from his body. When his muscles were as sharp as his mind. When he could go down swinging, then curse loudly at such rotten luck, because at least he'd have another chance, at least he'd play in a million more games.

John looked down at his hands, holding tightly to the chair, strength long turned to wrinkles. There was a time he was good at the game. Perhaps if he had worked harder.

Still, he couldn't shake last night. He should have nailed that ball. But, he didn't. And now he could only mumble to himself.

"It was only a dream, you idiot."

# CHAPTER 7

Monday, December 6. Shelly was driving to Escondido, her mind busily rehashing strategy.

She was confident for the second meeting with John, prepared with questions, angles, and a plan. She would be calm and sincere with her delivery, yet strong enough to push John into opening up before the camera.

Well, she didn't want to scare him, but she did want the interview to have some snap and power. It would be her task to expose both the mystery and true character of this man, and ultimately piece the puzzle together into a documentary masterpiece.

To her thinking, the account of John's life just might be of great historical importance, well beyond the already rabid countdown to Year 2000. And while the Millennium was being churned in ultra-hype as some sort of Mardi Gras on a double dose of acid, John Hammond's story was something far deeper—he had a chance to be remembered. This one man had not missed a moment of the 20th century. Technology soared and society continued to crumble.

Social commentary? Dead celebrities?

Perhaps she was getting a bit carried away with that angle. Wasn't it John who said the foundation of *The Brave Historian* was that the past wasn't that important anymore?

95

Still, what about John's friends when he was growing up? Who were they? What does he remember about them? How did they die?

There seemed to be a hundred possibilities to this story, though Shelly knew she'd have to cut it down and keep it clear. "Be sure to uncover the heart and soul of your subject," she recited aloud from some old college textbook, "but never confuse the viewer."

Simplify the complex.

\* \* \* \*

"Before we start, there's something I'd like to talk about," said Shelly.

"No problem," said John, thrilled that she had returned.

"I loved our interview the other day," she said. "You were great and it plays really well on film. The only thing I wasn't particularly pleased with was my questioning."

John looked puzzled.

"You have a wonderful story to tell," she continued, "but I thought my questions were just too shallow. The interview left me wanting to know so much more about you and I apologize that I didn't ask more pertinent questions. I left too many gaps."

"I didn't read it that way at all," said John, still bothered by his failure at the plate. How did he miss all three pitches?

He paused momentarily. There was a sweet fragrance in the room that suddenly struck fire to his senses. The smell of this woman brought a surge of power into his being. If Shelly had been in his dream, he would have demolished that baseball.

"I think you're being too hard on yourself," he continued. "It's difficult being on top of your game all the time."

"Or finding the perfect question at just the right moment,"

she added, unaware that splash of perfume applied four hours earlier was turning the old man into a wild wolf hound.

Settle down, John told himself. She was so beautiful.

"It just doesn't always seem to flow," she was saying.

"Hey, except on the best of days, my answers aren't that sharp anyway," said John. "Believe me, I can be a verbal vegetable."

"You're great at speaking," she said. "It's very dynamic. You, Johnny, have got the talent."

She expected him to smile, that she had recalled a piece of his childhood. He didn't.

"No," he shot back, a momentary pause in the back of his mind desperately attempting to block his father's memory.

"I think my mind is always far too busy for me to speak with accuracy, or even intelligence. Under any kind of pressure, the words get jumbled and I become even more rattled. I would much prefer to write my conversations down, then be able to erase the various mistakes. To speak to my potential, I would probably need five or six drafts to avoid sounding like an idiot."

"I think you're selling yourself far too short," she kidded.

"Wouldn't be the first time," he said, quietly realizing she had just nailed the story of his life.

"So, what's the plan?" he continued.

"Well, I just think I'd like to know so much more about you," she said. "And I'd like my questions to be more powerful, to inspire an honest comfort zone for you to be yourself."

"Okay," he said. "I'm already feeling comfortable."

"Wonderful," she said, stretching to touch his hand.

His breath was gone, but he hardly noticed, his focus captured by the unexpected feel of her fingers on his hand.

"I'll be honest with you," she continued, casually pulling back the distraction. "I was only asked to put together a few minutes on film. It really didn't have to be anything creative or special. What Mr. Stroud essentially requested was just an ordinary interview. But, now, I don't think I'd be satisfied if I didn't probe deeper into your life. You can stop me if that makes you uncomfortable. But, honestly, I'm not trying to dig up dirt or anything like that. I just find you very interesting. I hope I'm not being too forward."

She wasn't. John was once again lost in her presence, no doubt agreeable to anything she might ask of him.

"Probe as deep as you'd like," he said. "I've pretty much exhausted all my vanity. Really, I've got absolutely nothing to hide."

John thought about changing that last statement. He had plenty to hide. But, what difference did it make now? Maybe a shot of honesty would pump some life back into the muddy bloodstream. Plus, he felt so extremely young around this woman, as if he had just shed 70 years. Young and strong and focused on what he wanted and needed.

Relax, he thought. Slow down, be careful, don't say anything foolish. He noticed Shelly was still talking.

"Good, because I would like to get inside your head," she was saying, oblivious of where his mind was now wandering.

What Shelly did realize was that, for the first time, she was sounding bold. She liked it. As did John.

So why not push it one more level?

"As I said, this was only supposed to be a simple project," she continued. "I have not yet spoken with Mr. Stroud about my idea. I thought it was more important to talk with you first."

She noticed John was staring at her, probably losing interest in what she was trying to say.

"I'll get to the point," she said. "I would like to do an extensive documentary about your life."

John blinked and slowly changed position in his chair, trying to make movement appear much easier than it felt.

"I would like to talk about your family and the friends you grew up with," she continued. "I want to know about the best moments of your life and even the worst. I want to know what you were like as a young boy."

A young boy, thought John, what was that like?

\* \* \* \*

Shelly *was* tough. She stormed right into the delicate issues.

"I sensed in our first conversation that you really didn't want to talk much about your family. Why?"

John pulled back. No, he didn't want to discuss his family. Why did he agree to be open? Now he felt obligated, at least to say something.

"My family seems very distant now," he said.

Shelly smiled, waiting for more.

"There were times, when I was a young boy, I thought we were a perfect family. To me, there was no other family in the world, no other place I would rather be."

John's words were slow and distinct. His face was without expression, an actor who had rehearsed his lines far too many times. Then again, it felt good to finally talk, as if an infection had finally cleared, the fever broken, life renewed.

"I can still remember my father pulling away from the piano and saying, 'Let's tell some stories.' He would start one and then we'd all take turns in the creation of some fantastic tale. You have to realize that there was no television back then, no radio. We worked hard at our chores, but we always had time for music and games and fun and faith. It was as if we were all in the epicenter of life, together. Our imaginations seemed to weave a bond that would undoubtedly last forever."

"It sounds like your family was very close," said Shelly.

"There was respect and a good amount of love. Time moved slowly, life seemed very casual. There were moments when I truly believed that nothing would ever change. But I was certainly deceived. Things happen, people fall apart."

"When did it change?" she asked, glancing at the camera to check again if it was operating.

"I don't really know," he said, but his mind was taking him back to a pile of wood and a distant summer day.

\* \* \* \*

July 3, 1910. A Sunday, warm and fresh with a touch of approaching humidity. The day stuck in John Hammond's mind as if it were being replayed within a mystic haze. Perhaps it had always carried a surreal taint.

After church, Mother had prepared a picnic that the family carted to the edge of the pond that was situated near the cottage where Father did much of his work. Several hundred yards from the main house, Father could hammer out his tunes without driving everyone crazy.

It was a beautiful piece of land down there, an open field running smack into a small wooded area nestled against the east end of the pond.

Father was in a particularly jovial mood that day, having just sold his newest music to a publishing house. Unwittingly, Father had the power to pronounce the mood of the entire family. His disposition was like a signal from which the rest of the world adhered. If he was happy, everyone was happy. If he was deep in thought and not to be disturbed, Mother was quiet and the children had better stay clear. Father never so much as even spanked one of his children, but his growl could last for months. This day, Mother was almost giddy with joy.

John was 10 years old, dreaming of playing ball with Christy Mathewson and the New York Giants, as if Matty would still be pitching a decade down the road. David had just turned nine and would sometimes dream of being just like John, but more often his plans revolved around being better than his brother. If Johnny wanted to play shortstop for the Giants, then David would pitch for the Pittsburgh Pirates. Certainly, he would strike out his brother every time, hopefully reducing him to tears.

"It's okay, big brother," he would sympathetically yell as John walked slowly back to the New York dugout. "I'm just better than you are."

Mary was six and, as always, not concerned with anything her brothers were thinking or plotting. She liked to build bridges in the mud, create tiny roads from the dirt.

Sarah was excited about the doll she had received earlier that week for her third birthday.

And so the day unfolded, the Hammond family about to be forever torn apart.

The brothers were playing catch. A wild throw by David had landed near Sarah, who was busy jabbering to her new doll.

"Watch out for your little sister," Mother scolded. "You boys go somewhere else."

So they had moved their game, arguing about who had the better arm.

Mary had decided to sit with Father, who was reading a book under a clump of trees that huddled near the water. There were soft dirt formations with plenty of small sticks and flat rocks. She was going to build a world, she announced. Father chuckled. His little girl was truly a building genius. If only the boys had such vision. They just wanted to play baseball, a silly game reserved for lunatics and ruffians. No future in that.

Working on her quilt, Mother was left to watch Sarah, as she most often did. But the quilt was finally completed and she wanted Father to be the first to see.

"Johnny, you and David keep an eye on Sarah," she instructed, as if they completely understood her request. "I'll be right back."

She headed toward Father and Mary. If anything had been wrong, or possibly different or strange, wouldn't there be a sign or a warning? Wouldn't Mother, or someone in the family, sense the danger?

"George, what do you think?"

"It's beautiful, Lillian, a work of art."

"Mother, look at the world I'm building," said Mary, pointing with pride to her carefully planned pile of dirt, rocks, and sticks. "There's houses and roads and people."

"It's very nice, Mary," said Mother, glancing back to where Sarah was playing. Except she couldn't see the child. Mother's eyes searched toward the boys, playing thirty yards to the west.

"Boys," she shouted. "Where's Sarah?"

Father and Mary were hardly paying attention, but Mother had that sudden hollow instinct, one speck shy of horror. Just beyond the boys was a pile of wood where the kids were not allowed, but the sun was blinding her view in that direction, so she could barely see . . .

And the world turned to slow motion.

Sarah was sitting at the base of the pile, tugging at a loose log.

"Sarah," screamed Mother as she began a breathless charge. "Don't move," she tried to say, but her voice wavered to an almost incoherent utterance of sound.

Mary looked up, Father turned in sudden fear, the boys

stopped their game. Mother was still running across the field; her legs weak, her mind in panic.

Sarah yanked the piece of wood from the pile, perhaps a chair for her new doll, one lone log becoming dislodged from the top and falling silently through the air, smashing into the temple of the young child's head. No cries, just a thud.

It was only seconds until Mother arrived. It would not matter. The child did not move, did not breathe, ever again.

Mother would never lose the grief, blaming only herself for the loss of Sarah. If only she hadn't finished that quilt at that very moment. If only she could stop time, turn it back.

That winter, Lillian Hammond caught a chill and pneumonia followed with a vicious attack. She had no fight. The family would never know a more surrendered death.

\* \* \* \*

Shelly was beginning to worry. She had asked John when his family had changed and he replied that he really didn't know, then nothing. It had been nearly a minute and he had not moved, only stared at the camera. Was he dead?

No, he was breathing, just not responding.

"John, are you okay?"

John blinked, his head bolting slightly back, then once again finding the camera with his eyes.

"Yes, I'm fine," he said. "I'm fine."

He continued.

"I suppose it was the death of my little sister that changed my family. She died in an accident just a few days after her third birthday. Mother was crazed in depression and guilt, but I should have been watching Sarah, not playing catch with David. I should have told Sarah to stay away from the woodpile.

I thought she knew it was dangerous. I thought she knew . . ."

"How did the others in your family handle Sarah's death?" asked Shelly.

"You would hope that a family would draw closer together in tragedy, but ours became untangled. It didn't matter that we lived in the same house or ate at the same table or read from the same Bible. Conversation turned bland, the details of our lives became very private. There were no more stories, no more singing, no more laughter. Like a billion other families, we just went our separate ways.

"Mother died a few months after Sarah. They're buried next to each other in a small cemetery by the church. I don't think Father ever mentioned either one of them again."

\* \* \* \*

In the corner of the bookshelf of his room, John kept two scrapbooks. Shelly had asked if he had any pictures of his childhood. Yes, he'd get them, then joked that it might take a few days to make the journey down the hall. Shelly would have liked to see his room, but thought better of asking. She waited.

John brought the first scrapbook, then returned for the second. The book was old and thick and badly faded. She carefully opened it.

Faces from the past. So strange to look at people who lived in another time, so very strange.

For an instant, Shelly recalled being alone upstairs in her uncle's farmhouse. She was maybe five years old. It was a very narrow, musty room with only a bed, a dresser, and a wooden chair. And hanging on the wall at the far end of the room was an ancient black-and-white photograph of a young man, dressed in farmer dungarees, standing near a weathered shed at the edge of a cornfield. He was thin and rugged, his features as hard as the life he must have lived.

It was her grandfather, the first photo Shelly had ever seen of a person who was now dead. In fact, he had died long before her birth. Shelly stared into the picture, both frightened and intrigued. She wondered, recalling a lesson she had learned in Sunday School, if her grandfather was at that very moment somehow looking down at her from a cloud in heaven? Or was this faded piece of photography all that was left of an existence forever gone?

That same feeling slightly brushed her senses as she looked through John Hammond's scrapbook. Who were these people? Which one was John?

He was back now with a much thinner book that he set aside before sitting down next to Shelly.

"I take it these are your relatives," she said, feeling somewhat awkward.

"Yes, but these are photos taken before I was even born," he said. "I don't even remember some of these people, but that's my mother when she was a child. And those were her parents, who both died when she was young. I have never known them outside of this photo."

"Your mother was very pretty," said Shelly. "So this must have been about 1870?"

"Close enough. My mother, Lillian, wasn't born until 1883. She was only 16 when she gave birth to her first child. That would be me. Funny, but it always seemed that she was so much older. Probably because she was always protecting me and telling me what to do."

What also formed in John's mind was that he knew nearly nothing about his mother's youth. The family stories were always initiated and guided by his father. Mother listened, but seldom spoke.

Shelly turned the page.

"In fact, there I am, maybe a year old," laughed John. "Hard to believe I was ever dressed like that. Sort of embarrassing."

"Then this would be your mother and father?"

"Yes," he answered, then turned silent.

"They were a very handsome couple," she said.

Nothing.

Shelly turned the page.

"This picture was taken in 1910," said John. "That's me, my brother David, my sisters Mary and Sarah."

Shelly stared hard at Sarah. She was a beautiful little girl, with the same huge grin in the photograph as her oldest brother, John. At the same time, David and Mary both seemed rather intense, without even a crease of a smile. This was an interesting photo; one Shelly would definitely use in the film.

"Over the years, this old scrapbook has been significantly condensed," John was saying. "Plenty has been lost or maybe just thrown away. This is all that's left."

There was the house where John had grown up, his father standing at the door and waving. There was John standing next to David, his arm resting on his little brother's shoulder. John had that smile. David seemed solemn, almost defiant.

Shelly pulled her eyes away from David to look at John once more.

"You were really a good-looking kid," said Shelly. And he was.

John began to blush, but quickly moved along.

"This is my favorite picture that has ever been taken," he said. "That's me and Christy Mathewson. I was about 13 and he was visiting Lewisburg during the baseball off-season. That was a big day in my life."

"I'm sorry," she said, "Christy who?"

"Christy Mathewson," John said, his voice raised in excitement. "Only the greatest pitcher in the history of the game. He played for the New York Giants from 1900 to 1916, winning 373 games with a career 2.13 earned run average. He's the only pitcher in history to win 30 or more games in four straight seasons. He won 37 in 1908. Hey, in the 1905 World Series, against the Philadelphia Athletics, Christy pitched three shutouts. He sort of invented his famous fade-away, the screwball. It's the opposite of a curve."

John stopped, but it was only for effect. He was on a roll.

"Christy was tall, handsome and the embellishment of sportsmanship," he continued, as if he just might cover birth-to-death in the life of a god. "They called him Big Six, The Christian Gentleman, or just Matty. He was immensely popular, baseball's first role model, a true national superstar. There wasn't a kid in America who didn't want to be just like Matty; and I was first in line."

Shelly listened, partially intrigued and just a little bit confused.

"Yes," she said, "I think I've heard the name."

John was moving his arm and hand, emulating Mathewson's delivery. If not for age, John would surely have enacted the entire windup.

"Christy had perfect control and a powerful intelligence. He believed in an ethical code of sportsmanship. He was competitive, honest and refused to play baseball on Sunday; except once for charity. Christy was just like Frank Merriwell, the fictional hero of *Tip Top Weekly*."

Shelly smiled. She had no idea who this guy Frank Merriwell was and had never heard of *Tip Top Weekly*, but didn't dare ask.

"Professional baseball back then was filled with ruffians and illiterates, but Christy brought the game to a new, respectable level. When the Hall of Fame opened in the 1930s, Matty was elected as a charter member, along with Ty Cobb, Babe Ruth, Honus Wagner and Walter "Big Train" Johnson."

John paused again. Perhaps he was getting a bit too excited. He took a long, needed breath.

"You may think it's a bit weird that I know so much about one person and, honestly, I've never given such attention to baseball statistics, but Christy Mathewson was a legend."

John yanked his head slightly back. Here he was talking to a beautiful girl and bragging about a dead baseball player.

"Okay, now I remember hearing about him," said Shelly. "I didn't realize he had such an impact."

"Just before I was born, Matty had gone to college at Bucknell, which was located right next to the Susquehanna River, about a mile from my dad's farm. Christy was back in town for a visit on the day this picture was taken. He was my boyhood hero."

That's rather obvious, thought Shelly.

"During The Great War, Matty was an officer in the Chemical Warfare Service," John continued. "He was 38 years old and didn't have to enlist, but he did. Ty Cobb also served in Chemical Warfare and always said he remembered the moment when Christy breathed poison gas during a drill. Matty's lungs were ravaged and he died from tuberculosis in 1925, just 45 years old. The entire nation grieved."

Shelly began to turn the page, but John put his hand in the way.

"When I would go home to Lewisburg, I would always visit his grave. It was as if he was an old friend now gone. But, really, the only time we ever met was that one day in 1913."

John moved his hand and Shelly quickly turned the scrap-book to another page where she spotted a photo of John in college. He was holding a bat and wearing a baseball uni-form with Bucknell stitched across the chest. There was also a short newspaper article with the headline, "Hammond Leads Bison to Victory." She focused again on the picture. He was tall, athletic and had the same smile. And the same eyes, such won-derful dark eyes. Geez, he was a good-looking guy.

John noticed Shelly's interest. He took pride in that photo. And this was a chance for her to see his youth, the strength he had once assumed would never falter.

"John, you were so handsome," she said.

Stunned by the raw, fiery sound of those words, John felt a surge of power return to his body. It was only for a moment, but it was there. And he hoped that maybe Shelly could still see a trace of that youth as she looked at him.

"There must have been 100 girls chasing after you," she con-tinued.

"I don't think so," he laughed, trying not to blush. "I was re-ally shy back then."

On the next page was another photo of John, perhaps in his mid-twenties. He seemed to be standing in front of an office building. Another photo had him sitting at a desk, his fingers on a typewriter.

"I had just landed my first newspaper job in Williamsport," he said.

For just a moment, a spark stirred deep within her body. It had the feel of a sexual urge, but the quickness with which it began and ended hardly made a dent in her conscious mind. Indeed, he had been an incredibly attractive man with a great body.

Stop, she insisted silently to herself. Most definitely, there was some subconscious sorting to be done. After all, this was just a photo. Why should it matter now what he once looked like? Beauty withers. And even though the character and heart of this man must still be wonderful, his body is an absolute wreck, covered with lines and splotches and cracks and stains. Whatever he was, he no longer is.

The thought was gone, dismissed. Perhaps there was a gulp deep within her soul, but she really didn't notice.

Then, suddenly, it struck again.

As she returned to the eyes in the picture—the eyes of John Hammond when he was her age—Shelly was once again nailed by the physical presence of what had been this man. Imagination exploded. He was beautiful. She was captured by these eyes and time be damned.

As if courting curiosity, she turned away from the photo, looking squarely into the old man's eyes. And the beauty was still there. It was tired, damaged and somewhat hidden, but it was still there.

"John, if I had been around back in those days, I would have definitely been chasing you."

She touched his hand again, then pulled back.

What was she doing? What was she saying? What was she thinking? What was wrong with her? He's 99 years old, for God's sake.

Wait, she thought, it was nothing. No doubt the entire episode flew right past him. He had no idea what absurd thoughts had just blazed through her reckless mind.

But John had noticed something, what he thought might be a tinge of an unprotected tenderness, not only in Shelly's touch, but also in the way she had glanced at him. And somewhere within his stray hopes, he took it as an encouraging sign that she would mention that he was once so handsome. Perhaps she might still see him that way. And if that was somehow possible, he wondered just how far her mind might wander.

Not far.

Shelly was past scolding herself for the momentary lapse of bizarre weakness and total insanity. No one need ever know.

Her fingers slightly stumbling, she turned the page.

* * * *

In the dream, they were living on the fender of a car, not certain who was driving. The ride had been smooth, pleasant. There was an occasional rut in the road, but nothing they couldn't handle.

John looked at the other people riding the fender. They all seemed very familiar, but he knew none of them by name.

The sun was shining and it was hot. On both sides of the road was a dense jungle. John could hear the sounds of wild animals, but they mostly stayed hidden. And then they turned silent, the sound of the car's sputtering engine now capturing his attention.

As the car approached the top of a mountain pass, John noticed that the light had faded, the sun suddenly vanished. In fact, it was quickly becoming quite dark and the car seemed to be picking up speed. The road was also becoming very twisted as they began a hard and bumpy ride down the mountainside. Too bumpy. Someone shouted at the driver to slow down, but there was no answer.

The jungle had been left behind as the car burned around sharp turns on a steep cliff. John held on, but others began to fall, plunging to horrible deaths.

"Put on the brake," he yelled, but it was now apparent the car was out of control.

Near panic, John somehow moved to the door of the car, pounding on the window. If he could help the driver, they would certainly be saved. He pulled on the knob, but the door was stuck. His body was beginning to feel weak, his strength nearly drained. It was all he could do just to hold on.

John called for help, but there was no one left on the fender, only he remained on the outside. Again, he realized that he needed to get inside the car. It was hopeless, he thought, except he now realized the window had been rolled down. Whoever was inside driving had finally come to their senses.

But the car was moving faster and time was running out. With all his strength, John crawled through the opening of the door and into the front seat. He would be the hero.

Except the car was empty, the steering wheel broken, the brake beyond repair . . . not even a seat belt.

\* \* \* \*

John awoke hard, startled. His shirt was wet, his body shaking, his mind seemed outside looking in, confused by its displacement. Where was his focus?

Only a dream, he told himself, nothing but a dream. But every detail was etched sharply into his brain as if it had truly happened.

Once again, it had seemed so real.

# CHAPTER 8

High school, back again.

With Katherine's help, John walked into the classroom a few minutes after the bell and found a seat in the back. He always carried a strange feeling about school; like he was about to be tested and had not studied the assignment and really had missed most of the classes anyway and now he was trapped.

John took a deep breath, thankful he was no longer fifteen years old.

\* \* \* \*

Daniel Stroud loved being a teacher. He could list the assets of what some considered a thankless career as good pay, great benefits, long vacations and power.

He approached his job with great seriousness. Without question, he viewed education as fundamentally critical to the future. He stood on the front lines of battle every weekday from 7:30 in the morning until 3:15 in the afternoon. The enemy was everywhere—parents with issues, school board members with ideas and students with head colds.

Teaching was his craft and passion. He often claimed that his style was unique and demanding. Every angle of the class hour was planned within what he defined as a "stiff flexibility of learning and compassion." He once bragged that he could "teach the best, motivate the laziest and smell a lie before it was halfway told."

It was, at times, difficult to build respect with his students, but Daniel ignored the seemingly inevitable discouragement and plowed forward. Even when he occasionally tore into a student's work, he always attempted to move with a touch of humor and the mutually understood purpose between teacher and pupil to both correct and improve. At least that is the way it seemed to him.

As for creating an intellectual fever within all of his pupils— sorry, it never happens.

This particular English class had no honor students, just a bunch of sophomores who, according to the placement tests, were not particularly gifted. But there were a few who might someday make an impact of sorts. Somebody in the class might show the potential he or she surely must possess somewhere inside their thick skull. You never know. All it takes is one great English teacher providing the proper inspiration.

And that was Daniel's job—to jumpstart a pile of laid-back Southern California teen-aged brains with the beauty of literature, the art of writing and the rules of grammar.

"We have a special guest today, but before I introduce him, I'd like to say a few words about your book essays," said Daniel. "The assignment, class, was to read R.M. Milton's *Attack on Pearl Harbor*. You were then to write, in your own words, some of the thoughts that developed in your mind while reading the five-page article.

"Let me just say that some of the papers were quite entertaining. Ben Bates, I especially liked yours."

All eyes were now staring at Ben—third row, fifth seat— whose face turned pale and flush red all at once. This wasn't happening. It couldn't be. Why was Mr. Stroud talking about him? What did he do?

"I appreciate, class, that Ben used many of his own thoughts. Plus, he meticulously adhered to the laws of capitalization and placed his periods correctly in all three of his sentences, although I am not certain what happened to the commas."

There was laughter. The students loved the drama when one of their classmates was about to be staked through the heart.

"And I don't mean to embarrass you, Ben, because this was not the worst paper in the class. But, if anything, it reflects that many of you took this assignment far too lightly, that perhaps you could toss it together under 90 seconds. Despite the effort, I know you are all anxious to hear what Ben has to say about Pearl Harbor. Let me read his essay."

*In 1971 the Japanese blew up Hawaii. It pissed us off so we went to war and built a bomb that would blow them up and make them surrender. And then we won World War Two.*

Some laughter, several snickers and a few kids ready to blitz out simply because there was excitement in the room.

"Right war, wrong year, Mr. Bates," said Mr. Stroud. "I trust it was nothing more than a typographical error, but Pearl Harbor was attacked on a Sunday morning, December 7, 1941. You missed it by thirty years."

Laughter filled the room. Ben Bates was a dope.

"As for the United States being, how did you so eloquently put it—*pissed off*?"

The students roared. This was getting good.

"You don't find that particular terminology in many historical documents. And I doubt you can even find the word in

115

this fine dictionary our school board has approved. But, you're right, there was anger. And, one thing about historians is that they do try to be objective. The Japanese attacked, we went to war and we won.

"Believe me, Ben, I am not trying to be unkind. But in writing about such a profound moment in history, I would certainly suppose your mind would zoom with interesting possibilities."

The class was listening, hoping Mr. Stroud would blast poor Ben a few more times.

"Listen people, December 7, 1941 changed the very course of American history. It was understood at that one moment in time that the world, in the eyes of Americans, would never be the same again. Life had abruptly veered to a new and frightening direction. There were good sailors at the bottom of Pearl Harbor, many of them just kids, maybe a few years older than you are now. Their bodies were blown in a million directions. All they had been or ever would be was shattered in an instant of horrendous insanity. World War II? The dead didn't even know it had started."

Daniel checked for expressions. Nobody appeared on the verge of yawning.

"My guess is that most of you had grandparents in that war. In fact, your very existence just might be based on one of your ancestors getting through alive."

Several students laughed and others followed, probably not sure what the joke had been, but not wanting to look lost. Daniel momentarily considered asking what was so funny, but he didn't want to lose his point.

"In December of 1941, after the Japanese sneak attack of Pearl Harbor, and for many months after that, the outcome of the war was in serious doubt. The United States had been king of the ocean, but suddenly our entire Pacific Fleet was in shambles. We built bunkers on our shores, certain the Japanese would attack the coast of California or Oregon, maybe even Washington. The government ordered a blackout of all lights at night, food and gasoline were rationed, women and people too old to fight went to work in factories that built bombs and guns and airplanes. Survival hinged on the war effort. The nation was gripped by a horrendous uncertainty as young men went off to kill and die. There was no escape from the fact that everyone's life was in jeopardy."

Daniel paused and looked around the classroom. He was beginning to lose his audience. He had realized long ago that teenage focus could be elusive. Beyond the upcoming weekend, nothing much mattered. And they seemed to wear that disdain proudly, with absolutely no sense for their place in time. Who cared what happened between 1941 and 1945? To these kids, history was a boring subject about a bunch of dead people, all of them losers. And now they had to write about it for an English class? That's not even fair.

Daniel tried to gain mislaid momentum. He also realized that his historical tangent was mostly meant to impress John Hammond. Except, even John didn't appear to be paying attention.

"World War II was less than 60 years ago, folks, but the rules of life were quite different," continued Daniel, head raised into the storm. "There were no computers, no televisions, no VCR, no Pearl Jam, no Madonna, no South Park, no Beavis and Butthead."

Laughter returned. He was winning them back.

"Class, what if it wasn't 1999? What if, by chance, we are now living in December 1941? The walls are crumbling. You can't ignore the war. There is no rest. A brutal and unfair death could happen at any moment. You are frightened and paranoid and angry, but your country must be protected. You must be brave and lucky and somehow survive. Not one of us, class, can escape history."

Daniel sensed he had captured their attention.

"Now, 58 years later, it's different," he said quietly, with the effect of a stage actor.

Third row, second seat: Joanna Cubbage was contemplating a new hairstyle.

Fifth row, fourth seat: Matt Sanchez was checking out Joanna Cubbage. He wanted to drill her so bad he couldn't stand it.

\* \* \* \*

John Hammond's mind had clearly been wandering. Usually, Pearl Harbor stirred a rush of strong and still frightening memories—the disbelief, anger, anxiety. He vividly remembered the exact moment when he heard the news on that Sunday afternoon. Today, he was barely listening.

And it wasn't that John didn't enjoy these visits to one of Daniel's English classes. He loved to talk about the newspaper business, about writing. Just not today.

For the entire morning, all John could think about was Shelly. He knew it was nonsensical, that there was no possibility for passionate love, but he couldn't help himself. He just wanted to be with her.

\* \* \* \*

"Attention, class, today I am pleased to introduce a special guest," said Daniel. "My good friend, John Hammond, will be talking with you about journalism and also disclose a few tips about writing. John is 99 years old and, until he retired, spent much of his life as a sports reporter, so he's got some fascinating insights into the world of newspapers."

A few of the students had not really noticed John in the back corner of the classroom, but 99 years old? That got a stir.

Fourth row, second seat: Billy Jordan was stunned. He had never seen anyone this old, except probably on TV. It must be terrible to be that old, he thought. What could you possibly do? Really, you just get in the way. This old geezer ought to just die and get it over with. What if he just keeled over right here, right now? They'd probably have to dismiss the class. "Sorry, the old man is dead. You kids have to go home early." No, they probably wouldn't do that. They'd just send everyone down to the cafeteria and tell them to work on their homework until the bell rang when they would be ordered to go to their next class even though they had just witnessed a tragedy right in front of their eyes. They should definitely be let out early.

First row, third seat: Sandra Martinez also was puzzled. Her grandmother was 80 and totally incoherent. The woman lived in a rest home and the family had to visit her one Sunday every month. What a bore. So what could possibly be in this old man's brain? And why wasn't he sitting in a wheelchair?

Having waded through the stares, John now stood at a lectern in the front of the room and began to speak.

"When I was your age, I struggled with writing. What to say, how to say it. Writing was hard."

Here comes another lecture, thought Sandra, who was busy composing a note to be quietly distributed to any interested readers in her section of the room.

> *I wonder if this old guy would like a date with my Grandma? She can't remember shit, so he might even get some.*

Sandra grinned to herself, picturing the old codger mounting her grandma in the rest home. She needed to add one more thing to the bottom of her note.

*He'd probably fall asleep right on top of her. How
hot is that?
Gross!!!!*

Sandra carefully folded the piece of paper, checked to see that Mr. Stroud was watching the old guy speak, and quickly passed it to Rebecca Brookstone.

"To communicate, to be creative, writing is like a puzzle," John was saying to the class. "To begin, you must realize that the first words and ideas that you jot down are only a draft of what you will finally write. Without anyone hanging over your shoulder and passing judgment on your thoughts or style, you just work your words until they are exactly what you want them to be. You might start by just scribbling some thoughts, write what's in your mind exactly the way you are thinking it. Then, go over it a few times to make it better. After a few drafts, you've somehow come up with a powerful sentence or paragraph or story, nothing like the mess you started with. As long as you don't worry about the finished product until you get close to having one, writing is really quite easy."

A few were listening, but not many. Mostly, the stares had already gone blank.

"Dead man talking," giggled Sandra in a whisper that reached half the class. John heard the mumble, but couldn't understand the words. Still, he saw an entire section of the classroom begin to chuckle and knew it was aimed at him. He felt somewhat violated, but continued.

"For example, when you talk, you've only got one chance," he said. "If you make a mistake while you're saying something, it's too late, you've already said it. But, the great thing about writing is that you can make an error and then erase it, keep working on it until it's exactly the way you want it to read. It may take a few attempts with changing and juggling your words, but you can always write precisely what you mean."

What the hell, thought Sandra, is he talking about?

There would be no questions.

Finally, the bell.

# CHAPTER 9

Daniel and John had been discussing The Brave Historian for about an hour, neither caring to mention the difficulty of two people working on the same project.

"It was just like you were saying to your class today," said John. "You offered those kids a sense of time and place. But I don't think many of them were listening to either of us."

"English isn't important to them," said Daniel. "In fact, anything that doesn't interest them or directly pertain to their immediate pleasure at any particular moment is of no value. As for history, anything that no longer exists is meaningless."

"It would probably make more of an impression on them if they weren't so comfortable in their lives," said John. "These kids catch a glimpse of survival, then change the channel."

John slowly rubbed his head, as if the warmth from his hand just might keep the blood flowing.

"We sound like a couple of cranky old men," he said. "Perhaps our presumptions about history are totally full of crap."

"Except that everything we are at this moment has been molded by history," said Daniel. "Therefore, it doesn't matter what people think about the past because they can never escape its results."

"Sound argument, Plato," laughed John, "but I'm just concerned that we are wasting good TV time trying to write this stupid book. There's a rerun of Cheers on tonight I can't miss."

"*The Brave Historian*," reminded Daniel. "We're talking about the book."

"You mean the history of the 20th century through the eyes of Robert Patterson?" John shot back. "A bunch of words from a teacher of the obsolete?"

"I'm surprised at you," said Daniel. "It sounds as if you're writing for an audience? Stop me if I'm wrong, but I've heard you say for years, probably to every class of mine you're ever visited, that good writers must stay true to their own thoughts. I believe, in fact, you used those very words today. You're the guy who always warns that a writer should never worry about what the critics think or how to impress the reader."

"What if there is no reader?" said John. "What if nobody buys the damn book?"

"Then we blame it on the publisher," said Daniel. "They should have taken out some primetime television advertising."

"Excellent point," added John. "Maybe some poignant mass marketing campaign that features several extraordinary ladies sunning themselves on a beach, wearing skimpy bikinis, sipping lemonade and rubbing suntan lotion on various parts of their Playboy Magazine bodies while reading the blockbuster novel of the summer, The Brave Historian, written by John Hammond and edited by Daniel Stroud, topping the *New York Times* bestseller list for the next 77 weeks, on sale now at your local bookstore or wherever important mind-bending novels are available."

"You should have been in advertising," kidded Daniel.

"Yep, one more career to keep me busy," said John.

\* \* \* \*

John had turned off the television. He had nodded off halfway through Cheers, but now was wide awake. Shelly would be back the next day and he couldn't help but think about the interviews. No, he couldn't help but think about her.

John put the music of George Winston on the stereo, from a compact disc called *Forest*. He closed his eyes, quietly listening as Winston's piano produced *Walking in the Air*, a soft and wondrous piece of music that had been the theme of a video called *The Snowman*. For a moment, John wished he could still find such magic within his piano. But his mind was soon captured by the simple eloquence of the song. He loved this music. And if the folks from *Billboard Magazine* ever called, John would certainly list *Walking in the Air* near the top of his chart, right up there with Cat Stevens' *Miles from Nowhere*.

John had no problem being a fool for music charts, continually listing his all-time favorites as if the order was of great consequence. Nat King Cole, Doris Day, Perry Como and a thousand more great singers had each spent quality time at the pinnacle of John's private hit parade. Music from the '10s to the '90s, the sounds as diverse and scattered as his life.

Earlier in the day, he had been thinking about the Drifters, having a difficult time deciding which of their songs he liked the best, a battle between *Save the Last Dance for Me, Under the Boardwalk,* and *Up on the Roof*.

As for this moment, *The Snowman* created a different awareness. It seemed to glide John to another dimension where the cold and dark night was invaded by the tender light from a billion stars. And to the purely-formed imagination of one young boy, the fresh blanket of snow mixed magic with the wonder of life. The music captured all of his senses.

Without effort, John lost all thought. Now, it was quiet.

\* \* \* \*

In the dream, first his eyes and then his mind became extremely heavy. Ever so slowly, the world became quite dull. And he didn't seem to care.

John was traveling with a band of friends. Jessica, his wife, was an artist, a painter of strange and profound images. In fact, this was an entire group of artists.

They had sailed somewhere past the South Seas, but there was darkness all around them. They had stopped to paint in a small restaurant when John noticed Shelly walk into the room and take a seat at the far end of the table.

Everyone was eating, drawing and laughing, but John's eyes could not escape Shelly's.

Since his early teenage years, John had always had trouble looking directly into the eyes of a female, as if that would be invading her privacy, as if it would not be proper. He'd look at a woman, she would look back and he would look away. He had all sorts of lame excuses he regularly told himself about why he was so deficient in this most important social requirement. What could he do? Mostly, it had become a bad habit he was certain could never be broken.

But not now. He couldn't take his eyes off Shelly and she was staring back. He felt strong and confident as they had completely united into one another's presence. He moved toward her, electricity surging through him. She smiled, her eyes never faltering.

They talked for hours, for years, he wasn't certain; except that he deeply loved her and she loved him. He was dazed by her beauty, her smell, her voice. Never had he felt such powerful emotions for anyone.

But his friends were now leaving. They paused at the doorway to look back at him, obviously disturbed and wondering what he was doing with this young and beautiful woman. Yet, no one said anything until Jessica approached from behind.

"It's time to go," Jessica said, her voice abrupt and defeated. She was a tragic presence.

"Go ahead," John said, without looking. "I'll catch up."

This was no time to talk with Jessica. She was no longer his concern. In fact, he was rather angry that she would interfere. Didn't she understand that Shelly was the only woman he could ever truly love? How could he be bothered by anything beyond Shelly's beauty?

Jessica left and he did not notice. Only John and his love remained.

"I am expected to go," he said to Shelly.

"I love you," she said, "I will think of you always. And we will meet again. It has to be."

"Yes, our love is too strong," he said. "I must stay with you. I'll go to the boat, get all my things and be right back. It will only take a moment."

He tenderly touched her face, kissed her lips. She was all that mattered, all he would ever want.

He left to find the boat, but was suddenly concerned that he might be traveling in a different direction, headed down a narrow dock that was becoming consumed by a thunderous ocean. He could barely see, and tried to shout, but the noise of the waves was too loud.

He moved his head quickly, his eyes darting in all directions. There it was, he could see the boat, his friends waving for him to hurry. They held out their arms, somehow grabbing him from the ocean's power.

"I cannot stay, I must return," he told them.

But the boat was larger than he remembered and he had forgotten where his belongings were stored. They had to be somewhere. He anxiously searched a room that had once belonged to him and his wife, Jessica watching from a corner.

"Where are my clothes?" he demanded, no time to talk about anything else she might want to discuss.

"I don't know where you left anything," said Jessica, still bitter. "And it no longer matters to me."

Nor to him, for his search was now near panic.

Finally, there were his clothes, already neatly packed. He closed the suitcase and quickly walked past Jessica. Their eyes did not meet, their hearts held no connection.

He had to hurry, to return to his true love, but now the storm had taken the boat far from the dock. He tried to search for land, but the sea was too rough and he was thrown to the wet and slippery deck, unable to stand.

Much later, when the waters had calmed and a trace of light could be seen to the east, he returned to the restaurant, but it was empty.

Where was Shelly? This could not be. Why would she not be waiting?

John twitched violently, now beginning to realize that this was just a dream that would soon be over. In desperation, John tried to picture Shelly's face, to feel her warmth, to lunge for the very thought of her.

Try to relax, try to return. Too late, gone again . . .

\* \* \* \*

A thin strand of sunshine tore through the window shade, creating a streak of bright glare across a collection of old photographs that were framed on the dresser.

John was awake now, or at least seemed to be. Yes, because there was an irritating spasm between his shoulder blade he had not experienced in quite some time and now he noticed that his left arm felt very strange. What was that? There seemed to be another problem, a dull pain in his chest.

Uncertainty crept in without warning. He had battled this fear a thousand times. No, cut it off now. Keep the nerves under control. Don't think about death. Besides, it's way too late to worry. Perhaps he should just welcome it, just cave into the reality that there is no possible escape, that death is forever blank, forever nothing.

No, that can't be real.

If only he knew the future, it would be easier to plan, to protect himself. He also wouldn't have to worry about the present, especially if he understood that this was not really the end, that he would survive. He took a slow, deep breath.

Maybe he just needed to burp.

Anyway, this was not the time to think about his feeble body. There were other things to consider. That dream had been so real. But, even more significant, he had felt such a strong attraction to Shelly.

Perhaps another man might pass right by her without even a glance, but John was stunned by her presence. The strange gnawing in the pit of his stomach was a true sensation, and it was good. No, it was quite ridiculous.

John realized he was undoubtedly destined to bounce between feelings of love and frustration, but Shelly was so undeniably beautiful to him. It had been decades since his body had felt this way. He assumed it was no longer possible. But just to lay with her, to feel her firmness, her youth. It would certainly revive his life, provided he could survive the pressure. What would he do with a woman like her?

"I would swell and explode," he boldly proclaimed to himself. "I would thrust into her with power and passion."

He could feel that lost sensation. There was life down there, he knew it. And a strong sexual, erotic urge took hold. My god, was he getting hard?

Maybe not.

But, truly, his feelings for Shelly went far beyond sex. Their relationship was a matter of profound tenderness and understanding. If souls could fall in love, there was hope.

Then it hit him. What about Jessica? How could he have been so cruel to his wife? He had no right to betray the woman he had so truly loved. It didn't matter that she had not been alive for half a century. Even if it was just a dream, it was terribly wrong to be unfaithful. Sorry, but there could be no excuse. Shelly was just a fascination. Besides, he had been through the absurdity. It was not love, there was nothing to pursue, just forget about it.

But then he remembered her touch, her smell, that look she gave him for just an instant, the desire he had not felt for such a long time.

The pains had subsided. He slowly moved his arms and stretched his fingers. The nerves felt somewhat soothed, the muscles began to awaken. He took a deep breath, once again welcoming the calmness.

Shelly would return this afternoon. He was anxious to see her again.

\* \* \* \*

John's mind had returned to Jessica.

In the early days of their relationship, he had felt as if he had won the prize for loving the most beautiful woman in the world. It was sort of silly and he never told her, but he felt privileged to be with her. If she had any faults, he could easily ignore them. He saw only her beauty and kindness. It was as if his life was destined for her love. And they built a lovers' bond that would never die. The baby was proof of that union.

It was the best of days.

But, now, he was tired.

It had been more than 50 years since he had made love with Jessica. He tried to picture the last time, but could not remember.

Before the baby was born, their love had been passionate, as if they were perhaps the best lovers in the world, though he certainly did not fool himself into believing that kind of nonsense. It was just that he wanted her so much, and she the same with him. It was deep and forever . . .

And even after the baby was born, their passion at times raged with heat and fulfillment.

But then it ended so quickly, so hard, their love forever plunging into death, like a body from the sky . . .

Nothing really mattered after the fall.

Of course, they tried to make love, to bravely hold each other, but passion had turned to despair, the touch of her skin an invasion of lost and crippled souls.

Jessica built walls around her heart. And that is where she hid—hurt, afraid, devastated. As for the man she loved, she simply locked him out.

For a while, John figured it would just take time to heal, that he would eventually break through the unbearable fortress and bring her back, for their love had been too strong.

But he was wrong. He failed to truly understand her mind or calculate her direction. In her desperate search for their lost baby, she had already left him far behind.

\* \* \* \*

John had planned to take a brisk walk, but it was too cold to go further than the front sidewalk. He immediately returned to the house, uncertain whether to write, read, watch TV, or listen to music. So many choices, yet none seemed particularly appealing.

His best option would be to close his eyes and let the universe come to him. He still had several hours until the interview. He should just relax and feel what might unfold, perhaps to drift . . .

\* \* \* \*

Inside the dream, John was telling Shelly about the precarious state of his mind. As always, she was beautiful and caring.

"Just lately, my dreams have become real," he said.

"What do you mean?" she asked, her voice showing great concern.

"It's more than just remembering them," he said. "It's like I'm living inside each of my dreams. It's as if they actually exist."

"What do you suppose it means?" she asked.

"I don't really know," he told her. "Perhaps it is a sign that finally I will die. Or perhaps a brain cell has electronically malfunctioned and accidentally triggered the whole system into a complex hallucination that only appears to be tangible."

John was impressed that, within this dream, he could speak with such astute logic and intellect.

"Your mind might be playing tricks," Shelly said, obviously sympathetic to his plight.

"Maybe so," he continued, "but it's always an adventure and mostly I am young again, so I'm not complaining."

"You have always been young to me," she said, suddenly looking very seductive.

"Sometimes you are in my dreams," he said, looking directly into her eyes. "And we are lovers."

She came to him that night. He was young, she had strangely turned old.

"It's me," she said. "Don't be fooled by these lines."

\* \* \* \*

John thought he was awake, but could not be certain. He looked around the room, but there was no furniture and the walls were drab and blank. There also were no windows, only a door in the corner. Through the opening was a stairway to yet another room.

It also was empty.

\* \* \* \*

John shivered. There was a chill in his room and the radio was getting a fuzzy reception. He was awake and certain he had just been through an interesting dream but could not remember any of it. For a moment, there was a trace of remembrance. Something about intelligence, an old woman, and perhaps it was sexual. No, he couldn't quite get a grasp of it, recollection just out of reach. He stubbornly kept trying to search his mind for detail, but there was simply no evidence of what the dream might have been. Whatever it was, it had now completely disappeared.

It might be good that I have forgotten, he thought. That's the way dreams are supposed to work. Maybe I'm returning to normal. I just need to rest for a few more minutes.

Still, he once again attempted to capture what had surely been inside his mind and must still be there somewhere, but he had no luck. All he kept remembering was the dream he had experienced the night before. The group of artists sailing the South Seas, discovering that Shelly loved him as much as he loved her, and how Jessica had tried to interfere, foolishly trying to stop them, and just how easy it had been to finally leave his wife.

\* \* \* \*

The telephone had been ringing, the tape now picking up a message. Hearing Shelly Kingston's voice, John quickly tried to move toward the phone, hoping not to hurt himself in the effort. He fumbled the receiver, but managed to pick it up.

"Hi Shelly," he said, courageously trying not to sound short of breath. "Sorry about the tape."

"That's okay," she said. "I hate talking to those things anyway. Listen, the reason I'm calling is about today's interview." Don't cancel, he thought.

"I was wondering if we might do something a little different," she continued.

Thank goodness, he thought.

"Sure," he said, hoping she might want to include sex. She didn't.

"I want to bring another camera person with me today," she said. "I think it would allow for a few different angles to the story. And, also, I was thinking you might play the piano for me. I'd really like to hear you play some of your music. It would be great to film."

There was silence on his end of the phone. Sex would be better, he thought.

"I haven't played for quite a while, Shelly. I'd be way too rusty."

"It doesn't have to be rehearsed," she said. "I'd just like to hear some of your original music. And I think something at the piano would add a lot to what we're doing for the film. Really, it will be fun."

Fun?

"Sure," he said. "Why not?'

He wanted to say no, but couldn't refuse her.

\* \* \* \*

John had two thoughts crashing simultaneously through his head. Actually, they were more like emotions, both of them strong and slightly sickening. First, what was the deal with the piano? Why did he agree to make a fool of himself? He should have simply told Shelly that for a man of his age to play a complex musical instrument was not practical. He should have told her it would be far too strenuous, that he wasn't prepared. He hadn't played the thing in weeks. He needed to practice.

At the same time, he also could not shake that reckless dream about Shelly and Jessica. How could he be so unfair to his wife? He loved that woman and always would.

And, certainly, if he could somehow steal back one cluster of his life, just five years to live again, he would surely take the early years with Jessica. She had been the one to pull at his heart, to burn passion with romance. She was poetry, eternal beauty.

"I can just see you as an old man," Jessica had kidded him one day when he complained about a sore shoulder. "Naturally, I'll still be beautiful, but you'll be an old grump."

He remembered she had kissed him sweetly on the cheek, then tickled his ribs.

"Even when you have no hair, no teeth and can't hear a word

134

I say," she added, "just know I will love you forever."

And they created life. In every definition, their child was beautiful and precious, their marriage was perfect.

Then disaster, their hearts torn apart. He needed her, but never spoke. She needed him, but somehow could no longer touch.

And then she left him, as if their love was but a phase that didn't work out, as if that love and all its passion had grown old and sour and was ready to die. Hell, it was already dead, so who needed it anymore.

Certainly not her, not her.

John winced, once again recalling the careless note Jessica had left on the kitchen table.

> *I'm so sorry, but I just can't be here anymore. I truly did love you.*

\* \* \* \*

John was numb that January night in 1951. Despite the confusion and despair, he had not considered such a possibility.

How could she leave him? Before Sarah's death, they had been totally in love. With time, that love would come back. He had been as guilty as Jessica in shutting the door on each other, but somehow their love would once again be strong.

Yes, Jessica would return. She'd just walk in the door and hold him tight, say she was sorry for not confiding in him, that she would never leave again. Jess would come back.

It was late, Patti Page singing "Tennessee Waltz" on the radio, a sudden knock on the door, two policemen, uneasy in their manner.

"Are you John Hammond?" the officer asked. "I am afraid I have terrible news."

Once again, the entire universe crashed.

# CHAPTER 10

Shelly stood at the door, John trying hard not to stare at her beauty.

"Hi John," she said in a tone someone might reserve for the best of friends.

And there again was that hint of Jessica. Yes, not just the eyes, but the smile. He wanted to touch her, to hold her close to him, to let her know he had missed her deeply. It would not be appropriate, he realized.

"Shelly, good to see you."

He hadn't noticed that someone was walking up behind her. A man in his early twenties carrying camera equipment.

"John, this is Don Perricelli," said Shelly. "He'll be working the camera for me today."

"Hey John," said Don, not certain whether to shake the old man's hand for fear of breaking something.

"Don's a film student at UCLA," said Shelly, suddenly aware that John appeared somewhat anxious. "We've worked together on a number of past projects."

John's mind was once again carelessly racing. Who the hell is this intruder? Could this guy be her boyfriend? No, of course not. He's just a business associate. Film people work together all the time.

"Come in," said John, cautiously pulling back, out of the way.

Don was strong, lifting the equipment with relative ease. He also was good looking, but young. Certainly, too young for Shelly.

Get back to earth, John thought to himself, just slow down.

\* \* \* \*

Attempting to ignore the camera, John focused his eyes and mind on Shelly.

"The problem with these interviews," said John, "is I'm afraid it sounds like I'm bragging."

"Don't worry about it," said Shelly. "It really doesn't come across that way at all."

"I just wouldn't want to give the impression that my life has been some sort of great adventure," he added.

"John, the show is about you," said Shelly. "Just be yourself."

"Okay, ask your questions," he said. "I'll try not to stray too far from the truth."

Shelly looked at her notes.

"If you could retrace your life, what might you do different?" she asked as two cameras rolled.

John winced, silently sorting through his ancient pile of hopes.

"Tell me just a few," she prodded.

"Maybe I would have ignored the negative thoughts," he said, already perturbed he had agreed to be honest. "I definitely would have been more confident, more adventurous, more direct, and ignored the part of my mind that kept pushing me to hide.

"I would have been a great writer with a quiet place in the mountains and another on the shore. I would get up every morning and create. I would have written tons of important novels and short stories. Maybe that's what I would have done. And just maybe the world would know there was a fourth Hammond."

"Does that really bother you, John?"

"I'm not jealous, just pissed," he snapped. "And angrier at myself than anyone else. I created this senseless excuse that I couldn't write and publish books because my brother had beaten me to it. Not that our styles are even remotely related, but I always reasoned that I would be intruding into his territory. And now, David Hammond, who's been dead since Christmas Day of 1944, is required reading in nearly every college literature class in the nation. Sure, he was good, but maybe I was better."

John stopped for a moment. Perhaps he was jealous.

"Anyway, competition isn't the issue," he continued. "I've always known my reasoning was total hogwash and I can't remember when I wasn't fighting myself for staying in the shadows."

John fidgeted, as if perturbed to be sharing such thoughts. Too late, he was rolling.

"Same with the piano. I could have tried to sell my music, but my father was the piano player in the family, so that job was already taken. And it angers me that I could never get past that hurdle. It was like a giant wall I had no idea how to climb. I could have just walked right around that imaginary barrier, but I didn't."

John clinched his lips and shook his head.

"That's a dumb analogy," he continued. "See why it's so much easier to be a writer than a talker?"

Shelly smiled at his honesty.

"Mr. Stroud told me that you are an extraordinary piano player," she said.

"Well, maybe a few years back," said John. "But, again, my father was the family musician, so I stayed away. Makes no sense."

"Did you play the same kind of music?"

"No, I never tried to play the same stuff he did. He was rock, ragtime, kaboom. He pounded and danced and laughed. It was always a party when he played. My music is quite different, softer and deeper. To be clear, there were days it was rather sloppy. But when it was working, I could play the heart out of that piano."

John stopped, gazed down at his hands. His fingers were long, but the agility had long vanished. The hands were dry and wrinkled, with veins that resembled a colony of worms. He rubbed them together, attempting to hide the ugliness within his grasp.

"This may sound a bit weird," he continued, "but it's true. When the music is right, you can almost believe in the impossible. There was this one song I used to play and I'd imagine the wind cruising the high forests, caught between the warmth of the sun and the cold of earth, as if the wind could think and feel and breathe. My father chased the wind, tried to twist it in a thousand directions.

"If you were to compare our music, I guess mine is more New Age. Or maybe Old Age."

Shelly laughed, even though the joke was lame.

John once again looked at his fingers, as if wondering what potential might still be available.

"I've written hundreds of songs," he continued, "and never tried to publish any of them. I somehow got too caught up in not knowing where to ask and worried I would be rejected anyhow. To answer your earlier question, I would have changed that about my life."

140

"Could you maybe play one of your songs for me?" Shelly asked.

"Maybe on a perfect day," he answered, then paused as if a streak of bravery had suddenly smacked his brain. I guess I could play a couple of songs, but don't expect too much. Don't expect magic."

He pointed at the piano in the corner of the living room.

"There it is," he said.

"I know," said Shelly. "It looks pretty old."

Oops, that was not what she had wanted to say.

"Not as old as me," he said, not even flinching. "I bought it brand new back in the early thirties. Real ivory with its own unique sound, deep and rich in a funky sort of way."

She helped him out of his chair, walked slowly across the floor. Don's camera followed their movement, an old man and a young girl, choice stuff.

She was there for support as he sat down at the piano, though he was quite capable. Still, her touch was soft and vibrant. He would never shove that away.

"I came up with this song a good ways back," he said. "It changes just a little bit each time."

Don't talk, just play, he thought to himself.

He put his hands to the keys, silently hoping this would be one of those captivating moments. He started to play, a bit hesitant. His fingers seemed stiff. He seemed to be hitting at the keys. Yet, she smiled and the camera moved closer.

The sound was shaky, the effort strained. The music seemed stale to him. This was not a good start. He silently scolded himself for the self-doubt. He'd been through this lunacy before. Just relax and play, you idiot. Hear each note, simple as that. Don't think beyond the moment, just feel.

At the edge of his sight, he could see Shelly. But, certainly, she would not tell him how very horrible this was sounding. She wouldn't do that; even though, yes, this was definitely a disaster. Why did he choose this stupid song? He had barely played it in years.

The sounds became more and more stagnant as his fingers now turned clumsy from his mind's uncertainty.

Wait, the last time he played this song, it was beautiful. Now, not even close. He could feel fever attacking his body, followed by an irritating sweat. He fidgeted for a moment, not wanting to stop, not wanting to admit failure. There was no choice.

He stopped.

Shelly held her smile, although somewhat surprised at the abrupt ending.

John's hands did not move. He would have to explain. He would need to think of something quick.

"It's the camera," he said. "I'm used to playing this alone. The camera and the lights. I can't focus, I can't find the mood. I apologize, it didn't sound that good."

"It sounded wonderful," she interrupted. "Absolutely beautiful. It gave me goosebumps."

"No," he said, "you're just being kind."

"No, really, it's amazing," she countered. "I wish you would keep playing."

"Well, maybe another time," he said in a broken whisper. "Maybe if there was no camera. You could tell your cameraman to leave. I would play just for you, no one else. No cameras, just us alone."

John could hear himself talking, but could not believe he was saying something so childish and inane. Tell the cameraman to leave? I would play just for you? Nobody else? Just us alone?

Shelly turned to Don.

"Could you take a break for a while?"

"Good idea," he said. "I need a smoke."

Don got up to leave, quietly flicking his camera so that it remained operative. Let it run, he thought. Just might get something good."

John didn't notice the camera was still filming. He felt his breath was returning to its flow. There was still apprehension, but he felt better, stronger. And, like a child who had just got his stingy wish, he was once again alone with Shelly.

Now the room was quiet.

"I'll play something different," he said. "This is called *The Sands will be Warm Again*. I wrote it about 40 years ago. It was one of those songs that just happened. Sorry, I'm rambling. I should just play."

John took a deep breath, closed his eyes, slowly touched the keys. And, yes, the sounds were smooth, powerful, wickedly beautiful.

John knew immediately he had regained the touch. The music controlled the air with a profound and gentle deepness. This was the true sound and feeling of his soul, he had found it again. He didn't need to think or ponder, the music just happened. He could play forever.

In his mind, John pictured Shelly. He smelled her scent, rode the pattern of her skin, felt her soul within his fingers. It was as if his body had become one with the keys, as if he had turned sound into the very essence of life. Time was lost as one song led into another. There was nothing else but her and the music. If only she could feel his purpose, his passion. If he could simply reverse time.

Shelly was stunned, her senses being teased and danced upon. She felt a hard gulp in her throat and a tender mist building in her eyes. This music was wondrous.

It was there, right where he needed to be, except now his

body began to feel the strain of age. He slowed, suddenly near exhaustion, not wanting to let go of the sounds. Finally, he stopped. As the last note faded, John looked up into Shelly's eyes.

She was entranced, as if she now knew his secret, that he loved her beyond all boundaries.

"John, that's unbelievable," she said in a voice that was as soft as a whisper. "So fine, so very fine."

She leaned over to him, slowly kissing his cheek. Her fragrance was strong, her lips so soft and full. And now her hand was on his shoulder, her cheek resting against his. Let her feel the same love as I do, he thought. Just let her hold me longer, closer. Just don't let go.

But she did. She moved away, her smile altering the path of a stray tear.

"So beautiful," she said.

And yet so sad, she thought. This man has kept his genius hidden for all these years.

And he was wondering if she might ever hold him again? But, it's the music she loves, he told himself, not me.

\* \* \* \*

Shelly was gone again.

What struck him as odd was that he could not remember hardly anything about the interview, except there was an unwanted cameraman. He did remember the piano, the horrible start and powerful ending. And Shelly's eyes, her beautiful eyes.

But, mostly, the recollection was strained and blurred, as if maybe it really didn't happen. Perhaps he only thought it happened. Perhaps it was a dream. He just wasn't sure.

But he definitely remembered a kiss. And she had told him

his music was beautiful. He could still feel her voice whispering in his mind, "So fine, John, so very fine." Hadn't she said that? That could not have been a dream.

He also recalled that she had said something about another project, that she was going to Los Angeles, and that it might be at least two weeks before she could return. In fact, she had asked him to leave open the afternoon of Wednesday the 22nd. Yes, he had circled that date on his calendar, *Shelly @ 2:30.* He must have written that note within the last hour, but the recollection was very hazy. It should be so simple, but he just couldn't remember. He was tired, that was all.

Just get some rest, he thought. But, had that really been what she had said? Another two weeks? Could it be that she was planning to be with that film student, Don? Another jolt of suspicion. And why could he remember the guy's name? Don with all the muscles and probably the brain of a 12-year-old. John knew what was on Don's mind. He hated the guy.

Even while his mind was shooting poison darts at the over-sexed camera guy, John realized he was acting like a foolish kid. I should be happy for her no matter what she's doing, he thought. It's absurd to be selfish, to mistrust someone I love so dearly. And it's way too late to matter.

What's wrong with me?

\* \* \* \*

John was awake now and there had been a dream, but he couldn't remember. Something about a barren neighborhood, moving one place to another. No, the thought was gone.

He laughed to himself. So, once again, dreaming had returned to its rightful place of unreality. He was back to a normal life where dreams are naturally forgotten. The confusion

145

between dreams and reality had only been a phase.

Except now he was slipping again.

It was a long ugly room with no windows or doors. John thought he had been walking with his daughter, Sarah, but apparently she had left to play, a thick layer of smoke making vision quite difficult.

John also figured that, except for he and Sarah, the room was empty. But now he saw a figure sitting silently at a corner table. Moving closer, John could see it was his brother, David, pale and stoic, a look of disdain.

On the table was a typewriter, but the keys were loose and kept falling off.

John also realized Mary was in the room, working on a drawing. He tried to get a glimpse of her work, but she had it covered with her arm.

And suddenly, John heard music. He turned to see Father playing a piano. John knew not to disturb him.

Looking around the darkened room, John was feeling awkward, as if he needed something to do.

"I'm glad you're here," said David. "I need your help."

John looked at the typewriter as it continued to crumble. He looked sharply back to his brother.

"I'm not good at fixing things," said John. "You should know that."

"The typewriter works fine," said David. "There's a couple of letters missing, but so what."

John glanced again at the typewriter, which now resembled a computer.

"What I need are stories," continued David, "I have absolutely nothing to write. The words no longer make any sense. They just hang there with no connection, no meaning."

"Writers always have hurdles," said John, as if he were once again the mentor. "Just take a deep breath. A good walk can do wonders."

"I don't need a walk," grumbled David. "I need ideas. You could always make up a good story. Father loved your stories."

John pulled back from the table, but Father had stepped up from behind and grabbed his shoulder. His hands were huge, his fingers long and powerful. He also was very young.

"Okay Johnny," said Father, "I'll start a story and you finish it."

Why was this man acting so friendly? For a moment, John felt a strong sense of trust and love, as if being hurled back to his own youth. But, no, that was not possible.

And then he remembered he hated this man. It didn't matter that his father was, at this moment, but a young man. It was what he would become, what he would do . . .

And John shoved his father, pushed him hard against the wall. As adrenaline roared, John pushed again, so hard that the wall collapsed to reveal a cliff with a drop that plunged forever.

They struggled, George Hammond's back braced on the edge, one slip to a brutal death.

"Don't do this Johnny," he yelled, his voice cracking, his eyes torn by fear.

John grabbed his father's neck, only to see the face turn swiftly from young to old; only the panic remained.

"You go alone, old man," screamed John as he shoved his father one last time, a withered body disappearing into the depths of darkness.

And there was justice, for the old man had carried only himself into death.

John pulled away from the cliff. It was a moment of intense emotion and satisfaction, as if he had finally changed the very course of history. Now, he just needed to find his daughter, to

147

hold the little girl in his arms. She had been with him a moment ago.

Where was Sarah?

He looked back into the room, but it was empty.

# CHAPTER 11

Shelly was deep in work—reviewing, editing, thinking.

She should have been packing, but tomorrow's trip to L.A. had barely crossed her mind.

"Two weeks stringing for a major TV station in Los Angeles," her dad had exclaimed, as if she had just won the grand prize of life. "Mom and I are so excited for you. This will be wonderful. You might even land a full-time position. You might even be the next anchor for the six o'clock news."

"Dad, they want my camera, not my personality," she had replied. "It's just temporary."

"Don't get me wrong, Pumpkin. I'm not trying to add any pressure, but this could turn into a huge opportunity. You never know what's around the next corner. You just go up there, work hard, have some fun and see what happens."

Well, that's exactly what she planned to do. And if something did break for her, she'd deal with it. But she wasn't about to get her hopes too elevated.

Don Perricelli had originally been offered the spot, but the college semester had just ended and he had arranged for a two-week trip to meet his girlfriend's family in Missouri. He had mentioned Shelly for the job—she knew the ropes and had a great eye. The guy from the station had seen some of her work and called immediately.

But Shelly wasn't thinking about *Action News* or the three-hour drive in the morning. She was more interested in John Hammond.

On her desk were John's two scrapbooks. She had expected him to be reluctant when she asked to borrow them, but he seemed more than willing.

"Take what you need," he had said.

Shelly looked away from the film and once again began glancing through the books. It would be super effective to weave some of these old photos into the film, but she was far from deciding any process or order.

The picture of John with his brother and sisters in 1910 was a definite keeper, as was the photo of him as a college baseball player at Bucknell. What a stud.

Let's not go down that path, she quickly thought.

But she did. Her mind began to wander and she did not stop it. What would it have been like to sleep with John Hammond in 1925?

Then her brain made a sharp turn that at first seemed almost amusing, but definitely dark. What would it be like to sleep with a 100-year-old man?

Make love? Could he even do that? It was physically impossible, wasn't it? She had no idea about such things, but it was probably all crumpled and, hell, he couldn't use the thing unless he was some sort of Superman. There just wasn't any way.

No doubt he was once handsome, she thought, but this is disgusting.

She should have stopped there, but now she was on stage with an excess of sick possibilities. He's just an old guy, probably horny as hell. And just think about the way he looks when he talks to you. He definitely wants in your pants.

Her mind repelled the image, yet it fought its way back carrying a quite different emotion. For an instant, they were touching, her body wanting fullness, his body so frail. Perhaps, he just needed to be held.

Think about something else, she told herself again and the picture vanished. Thank goodness.

But then another thought arrived that surprised her. It was a touch of guilt with a wallop. John was a kind and caring person. How very crude of her to think only in terms of age and skin condition and how his body had weathered. It's the soul of a person that dents the universe.

I'll bet there was a time when he was unbelievable in bed, her mind continued. But that would have been before my grandparents were even born.

"Think of something else, please," she stressed out loud.

Then again, what could she possibly say to the old man about what might have once been his sexual appeal? You know, John, you once were quite handsome, but now, of course, you're a mess.

Not that she would say it quite that way, but it was a fact.

Am I attracted to this guy? No, certainly not. Okay, at one time he was a beautiful man. You can still see it in his eyes. They are very powerful, very pure.

Stop.

She was building him into something he obviously wasn't. He was beyond old. It was just a pointless fantasy. It was simply not feasible.

It was not possible.

\* \* \* \*

Shelly's pretend seduction had been replaced by a self-imposed shame and admonishment. She felt unclean, lured to a place she did not like to frequent.

Any affection John might feel toward her could only be compared to a grandfather's love for a child. Most likely he saw her as the granddaughter he never had. Or, in this case, perhaps she would be more like a great granddaughter.

If her thoughts were a movie, she most certainly would edit the past 15 minutes, toss the evidence into a fire and slide effortlessly back to the good sense of her Christian faith.

\* \* \* \*

Shelly had returned her focus back to work.

"I could blend in his music," she whispered to herself.

In fact, the entire score could come from John's piano music. It would be perfect to have a tape of his music done professionally, but that might be too difficult to arrange and probably excessively expensive. Still, even what she already had on film could probably work.

It also hit her that despite nearly five hours of film, she had very little about John's family. He had talked about the deaths of his baby sister and mother, but not the others. John had really said next to nothing about David or Mary, even less about his father. Weren't they supposed to be the interesting ones?

"How dumb am I?" Shelly asked out loud.

They would be in the encyclopedia. She could undoubtedly uncover information on Mary in an American art history book. There also must be plenty of details about David's life. She could probably still find his books somewhere. And there must be music history books with something about George Hammond.

She had been so caught up in John Hammond she had failed

to do her homework. She could hit the downtown library when she returned from Los Angeles, then check San Diego State.

She never particularly enjoyed research because she had a hard time getting started, but this would be fun.

Then again, why wait? It proved a good start that her computer's encyclopedia was loaded with information about all three of the famous Hammonds. Of even more help, she found a link to a rather offbeat biographical sketch about the Hammonds in an old copy of *Intellectual Digest*, a magazine she didn't even know existed.

The article was a treasure.

*David Hammond was born on April 12, 1901 in Lewisburg, Pennsylvania. He attended Penn State University, but flunked out after his sophomore year for failing to attend classes. With a lust for wandering and a string of failed careers, he had his first novel,* Blue Gold, *published in 1937. While never a mainstream hit, the book established for David a strong cult following amongst intellectuals and bohemians.*

*Taking residence in New York City, David seemed to do his best work with a turbulent mind. In 1940 the* New York Times *quoted him saying, "My work is writing, my goal is to wrap the readers' minds in knots. But mostly I am interested in alcohol, drugs and women; giving me both purpose and misery. Thus, I always have plenty to write about."*

*With manners that ranged from blatant to rude, he was somewhat of a tyrant with few friends and a long police record, usually for public drunken-*

*ness or barroom brawls. It was in drinking establishments that he claimed to do his best writing. "I sleep where I drop," he once boasted.*

*David Hammond was obsessed with the realm between life and death. "I've been there and I've been back," he wrote. "Death is only frightening if you give a shit about life. I don't."*

Shelly wished she had kept her copy of *Blue Gold* from college. For some reason she had sold it back to the bookstore along with her textbooks. She did recall it was about a man's desperate search for satisfaction and how, the few times he did reach perfection, he could never make it last. At least that is what Shelly figured David Hammond was trying to say. Her professor had about 20 other themes and they were all on the final exam. Shelly got a B-minus on the test, which she considered a sure sign she probably had a reasonable grasp on David Hammond's obscure messages. After all, he was mostly writing in a drunken stupor, then editing when his eyes could focus.

*On Christmas Day in 1944, David Hammond, claiming to be losing his battle with insanity, typed an 80-page suicide note, then chugged an entire bottle of rat poison. The note was published as his 17th novel, which took its title from his final words,* Death Be but a Short Vacation.

John's sister, Mary, also was plagued with various mental complications.

*Born in Lewisburg on February 1, 1904, Mary Hammond graduated with honors from Bryn Mawr*

154

*College in 1925. Mary was often considered a surrealist, but her oil paintings also touched the popular school of social realism that flourished during the 1930s. Her sculptures were considered even more powerful than her paintings, being lumped anywhere from cubist abstraction to constructivism.*

*An extreme perfectionist, she had a number of emotional problems that would shatter three childless marriages while leading to several well-documented breakdowns.*

*On March 8, 1941, in her Boston studio, Mary Hammond completed a near-hypnotic painting she called,* The Search for A Better Lover. *Its title apparently led to a fatal argument with her jealous boyfriend, Peter Orwell. He later claimed she pulled a knife on him and, in self defense, he stabbed her 27 times, including five slashes to her throat. The boyfriend was eventually executed for her murder.*

*That final painting by Mary Hammond recently sold for $1.4 million.*

Their father, undoubtedly the inspiration for their madness, also made a solid cultural dent in the world.

*George Hammond was born in Lewisburg on July 30, 1871. Taught to play the piano by his mother, George had written dozens of songs by the time he was a teen-ager. The first published musical composition was "March Hard, March Strong" in 1892, written during his senior year at Princeton*

155

*University.*

*Hammond once said he liked to keep his "instruments busy and their sound wild with laughter." Too wild, for some critics, but the public loved the fun and excitement of his music.*

*After college, George moved to New York City for several years, but preferred to compose at his family home in central Pennsylvania, where he married Lillian Rogers in 1898. They had four children, including writer David Hammond and artist Mary Hammond.*

*George Hammond published more than 400 songs during the first 19 years of his career, but after the deaths of his youngest child in the summer of 1910 and his wife in the fall of that year, his productivity tumbled dramatically.*

*Despite a string of musical busts that seemed to silence his career, he notched a surprising comeback when he wrote and published* Soft Return *in 1947. A tender ballad, totally unlike anything he had ever written, the song remained at the top of the charts for several months and restored his popularity and fame.* Soft Return *was Hammond's last and, undoubtedly, greatest song.*

*His health failing, George Hammond committed suicide on April 2, 1950 by leaping from a steep cliff in Pennsylvania while holding his only grandchild.*

Shelly stared into the page, trying to sort through a horrifying jolt of existence, trying to sort truth from the unspeakable. It took a moment for her to realize exactly what she had been reading, a moment that was both dull and hollow, a moment that sucked all comfort from life.

Grandchild? What grandchild?

And then it struck her. This must have been John's daughter, Sarah. What was it that John had said on film?

*"It was 1950, like a hammer to the soul . . ."*

Shelly had uncovered one more piece of John Hammond's fragile puzzle. She was stunned, empty.

What could possibly have happened?

\* \* \* \*

John wanted the walk to be a bit longer, but his body was hurting in too many places. Now, he just sat in his chair and stared at nothing, his mind still trying to separate dreams from reality.

Sure, dreams sometimes seemed real, but not every time. And they didn't have the same kind of texture and substance as reality. But why was he remembering them with such clarity and detail? It didn't make any sense.

Of course, it might be the dosages of his medicines. But tell this story to a doctor and John would probably be prescribed five more kinds of pills. Talk with a psychiatrist and John would probably be told he was just losing his mind.

John could envision Daniel discussing the situation with Shelly.

"Medically impossible," Daniel would say, as if a high school teacher had access to such knowledge. "Dreams are not real. It's just his mind. This is what happens when the brain falls apart."

"His dreams must seem real to him," Shelly would say in John's defense.

"I don't doubt John believes it," Daniel would argue. "He's

old and unsure. Maybe things inside his head are getting a little rocky. Or maybe he's looking for attention and has made the whole thing up. People do all kinds of unusual things when their thoughts are cloudy."

But now John's fantasy has Shelly lowering her voice to a near whisper.

"I don't know, John looks really pale to me. His skin seems sort of gray and pasty. I'm worried for him."

"Well," Daniel would laugh, "it's a miracle that his body even works at all anymore."

Near anger, John snapped the imaginary conversation out of his mind, but continued to process the problem.

Perhaps the entire dream situation is an omen, he thought. Perhaps it's just another reminder of how the body withers and dies. What is strong will always turn frail. And so it must be with his brain. Death must be near.

"No, it's not that, it's got to be something else," he said to himself as if talking out loud would chase away the unavoidable.

John looked closely into the mirror. He kept looking older.

Perhaps my mind has finally popped, he thought.

Whatever the reason, there is nothing wrong with remembering your dreams. He appreciated this new dimension of his life.

On the other hand, he was beginning to lose grasp of what was real and what was imagined. He wasn't always certain whether he was awake or asleep. It was tough keeping track.

And, essentially, he would rather be asleep. At least there was comfort inside most of his dreams. He was young, he was more alive.

\* \* \* \*

John's mind returned to Shelly and the 14 long days without her. But, really, a couple of weeks out of 100 years is nothing, he figured. John did the math, realizing he'd already lived more than five thousand weeks. What's another two? He would just focus on his writing and not think about her at all. He would start immediately. No distractions, no television, no people.

He looked again at his calendar. Fourteen days.

\* \* \* \*

Shelly had been wrong about Los Angeles. Sure, it was a million miles of concrete and cars, but it burned with excitement. Her work was stimulating and the people she worked with seemed to thrive on the explosive pace. The news anchors were deeply in love with themselves, but at least they were fun. A string of shopping center thefts, police chases, gang violence, a botched kidnapping, a drug and weapons trial of a movie star—these were great assignments. The hours passed so quickly she hardly had time to enjoy the day.

The station also was running various human-interest stories related to the upcoming millennium celebration. Shelly realized her film about John Hammond would be perfect. When she shared John's story with the station's news director, Bob Beatty, he showed immediate interest.

"That's exactly the kind of thing we're looking for," said Bob. "Put it together and send it up."

No problem. She'd work up a three-minute segment about John's life the moment she got back to San Diego.

Bob also mentioned she'd be paid for the piece. Shelly was too thrilled to ask how much.

\* \* \* \*

John was stuck.

He had been distracted for days. It didn't matter what he was doing, he was obsessed with Shelly, continually twisting various scenarios as if fate could step up, do its job, and bring her back to him.

In his mind, John would time-travel back to her, or die and be reborn into another dimension where he could wait for her. Heaven? Another galaxy? He'd take anything.

Scientists would announce tomorrow they had discovered a drug that reversed aging so rapidly that a person could lose 70 years in 10 days. By the time Shelly returned from Los Angeles, John would be 29 years old. Best not to take too much.

Anyway, John was supposed to be concentrating on *The Brave Historian*, not thinking about Shelly. He had to get this thing finished. It's just that the words and thoughts weren't working.

There had been an interesting idea he had meant to remember, but had failed to write it down. Now it was forgotten, yet another brilliant concept that had passed through his brain and into oblivion, ideas he would never recall no matter how hard he pressed, as if Einstein had clutched the key to the universe and forgot to jot down the details.

The page was blank, John's mind apparently gutted. The whole thing, after all, was a lost cause.

"Nobody reads anymore," he mumbled to himself.

Besides, he had written all of this before. Plus, someone had most likely already had those thoughts. Today's bookstores were buried in a pollution of words, every creative idea already expressed a thousand different ways. Nothing new, it was all a senseless rehash. Why even bother.

For a moment, John thought of the times when his words seemed clever and his stories important. But, like always, his thundering surges of confidence were followed by devastating thoughts of failure as true genius turned to pure garbage.

His final move would be to once again place the pages back inside their tattered manila folder, bound for a cardboard vault.

Or maybe just destroy all of it; every thought, every word.

"Loser," he whispered. "You could've been so much more."

Perhaps if he just wrote down everything that came into his mind. Yes, a stream of consciousness to rediscover that creative spark, to write and not stop.

Thoughts were again storming through John's head. He just needed to relax and follow the words that he could shape like paint to a canvas.

And so he began.

> *The idea is to own a fast pen, to move quickly as to catch the brain off guard. Truly, the mind is only a storage tank of thought and nerve. It only pretends to be elusive.*

"Just write," he blurted.

> *You would think people who create would always find an audience. And those who copy would be exposed.*

Worthless dribble, he thought. Just follow your own style, don't worry how others might react.

> *We give the illusion of movement and intelligence, but our minds are separate and our thoughts never cross paths. Padlocked in mystery, the mind is a silent treasure chest with all outsiders denied access.*

*Best to keep all entrances closed and hidden.*

He had touched upon these ideas before, and his fingers hurt.

*Scribbled thoughts were alive with possibility, but he had left too much for another day . . .*

Change course, he told himself. Keep the pen moving and push for a different idea.

*Now the cold night rubs against my bones. My feet have turned cold, my eyes burning. Beneath it all is a drive to be loved, to be respected, to capture one last moment of youth.*

*No, I must admit I am old, that something unwanted is right behind me and quickly closing, an intruder whose shadow has somehow edged itself just inside my being.*

*And the old folks sit around with bodies that don't move and brains that don't operate. He's sharp, he's healthy, he's really slow.*

Sorry, but nobody wants to hear about your pains and you sure as hell don't want to listen to their health report. Plus, John thought, this stream of consciousness can either create magic or be a complete load of bullshit. He once again attacked the paper.

*The past had become vague and the future was limited. All the time, the old man was simply hiding a secret he had long ago forgotten, cloaking his own soul as protection.*

162

John paused, as if his insights might somehow have significance. But his mind suddenly wrenched and his body felt the
fall.

*All hope was now gutted. I had held back in hopes*
*that the bookshelves might rot by their own weight.*
*Damn the caution that killed me.*

It was now a struggle, words and meanings spinning in
circles.

*It just dawned on me. I write extraordinary books*
*with no intention of ever finishing them.*

He closed the notebook, leaving the pen inside. It was late
and he was tired.

* * * *

The forest was strangely silent to his presence. The trees
were stiff, their branches robbed of life by an uncaring winter.
No birds, no bugs, no savage game, just an empty void. Surely
he had hunted here before, perhaps killed.

But through an opening he noticed that the snow and ice
had melted, leaving the ground soft and green. There was a
warmth as he realized, for the first time, he was naked. And he
was young again, perhaps the perfect age. His mind was as it is
now, but his strength and vitality had returned. He was sharp,
he was strong. He gazed at his hands and they were smooth
with the sleekness of an animal in its prime.

And there was a woman.

She appeared after days in the sun, her clothes dried with a scent of perfume and perspiration.

"You are beautiful," he said with bold assurance.

She tried to look away from him, to present an air of mystery, but she could not avoid his eyes nor hide her needs.

"I have never loved a man so much," she said while moving toward him, her eyes fixed deep into his.

He gulped hard, realizing that this would be their only moment. He dare not lose focus, not even for an instant.

He touched her slightly, her gown falling to the floor. Her softness and smell were overpowering, her body aching with a wild and penetrating heat, her touch igniting a fire that swept them together, raging out of control within their very souls.

She was firm, he was hard, their bodies locked in both love and lust. He wanted to taste all of her and she did not pull back.

It struck him in this moment of perfection that somehow he had found the center of the universe.

And it was quiet with the noise of the night.

# CHAPTER 12

John lay quietly on his bed, moving his fingers slowly across his chest and groin like an animal savoring the thrill of its latest conquest. She had been beautiful and tempting and sensual to his touch. He had been strong. They had exchanged great pleasures and, certainly, she would want him again.

He wanted her right now. To see her naked in the daylight, to prowl into the warmth of her body. He had a dry, hungering ache for more.

But he now felt a different ache in his lower back. Damn, he'd twisted something. Just relax, don't stray from this moment.

Too late. Slowly, his thoughts were leaving and he could not retrieve them. This beautiful woman, who had shared with him an absolute intimacy, had quickly exited without the slightest remark. Now she was gone and he would never have her again.

John was frustrated, angry. If only he could have pretended for just a little longer.

\*\*\*\*

Shelly had thought about calling John to tell him that life in Los Angeles was busy and exciting, that she was looking forward to seeing him again, and that he might be on television. She meant to call but didn't.

****

John's mind once again drifted.

Other than his latest dreams, it had been years since he had slept with anyone. The last real time was a night in the early '70s with a woman he had met through friends. Now, it was a haze; at the time, it was a disaster.

She must have been in her late 60s, obviously self-conscious and uneasy about how her body had deteriorated.

They touched in the dark, each looking to be fooled. Her skin was soft and almost mushy, contours moving in directions that were not pleasing to his imagination. Even her kiss seemed dry and disoriented. It did not work, he could not be hard, they both left embarrassed.

He saw her several months later, but they avoided talking. She was certainly dead by now, the secret forever safe.

****

There was nothing to do.

Daniel, Katherine and Ashley were watching television. Actually, Katherine was reading the newspaper, rather oblivious that her husband and daughter were entranced in some stupid sitcom. John had wanted to join them, but his mind couldn't persuade his body to get up from the bedroom chair.

The kids, and their father, were excited because they only had two more days of school until Christmas vacation.

Zack had asked John to watch him play his new video game. It was something about escaping from a Nazi prison camp. Zack even allowed John to take a turn at zapping Nazi guards. The kid reset the game to the beginner level so that all the Nazis were now quite lethargic and John had an easy time shredding them with his machine gun. Only occasionally did he get killed. And that was his own fault, busted reflexes.

"You gotta be quick in this game," said Zack, taking over the controls and moving briskly to the expert level.

After Zack had racked up several hundred dead Nazis, John excused himself from the game. Entering Hitler's private chambers, Zack didn't notice John's slow departure.

Katherine was in the hallway. She immediately looked busy. Perhaps it was just John's imagination, but lately he'd detected something strange in her mannerisms he had never noticed. Not that Katherine wasn't polite; it was just that she had always been so kind to him, so relaxed in his presence. But more and more she seemed tense and not really caring to talk or even smile.

John needed to get back to his room.

On the desk, he noticed that Daniel had returned his latest chapter of *The Brave Historian*. "Excellent" had been scribbled in red across the top of the first page, as if this was a prize high school essay. John chuckled, half expecting to find it graded.

They had 87 pages now, 12-point type on the computer with double-line spacing. It wasn't even close to being completed, but at least there was progress.

John had been thinking about what Daniel had suggested. Perhaps he should explore and incorporate some of his previous writings into the body of *The Brave Historian*. That wouldn't be cheating. Writers did it all the time.

He would ask Daniel to go out to the garage and bring back several boxes at a time for him to review. To Daniel's thinking, it would be a sign that progress was being made. For John, it would just be a matter of locating and organizing. He could take what might fit, then weave it together as part of the overall puzzle. Besides, he had plenty of material to match the theme.

John reviewed the synopsis in his mind.

*A history teacher, Robert Patterson, realizes his life has been squandered. But there comes a time when every person must be bold, to carve their mark into the heart of the universe, or something like that.*

Of course, John still wasn't sure what course the story would ultimately take . . . a happy ending to soothe the reader or a tragic conclusion to fit reality.

****

John was wasted.

The entire day had been a strain. Hell, the thoughts he was having about Shelly were enough to kill a man of 60. He needed warm sand and sunshine. He needed to run, damn it.

He needed to make love with Shelly.

****

He was resting now, his body beaten. Still, his breathing was smooth and he felt rather calm. It had taken years for him to be able to rest without worry, to breathe deep and slow, the world no more than a soft darkness.

It had been quiet within the dream, but now the music was loud. John found himself in the center of the room, at one with his piano. He had planned to play New Age, but had been coerced into rock 'n roll.

The keys were blazing . . .

Fats Domino was watching from the edge of the piano. Fats

wanted to play *Blueberry Hill*, but the crowd favored John. A beat that had started from deep within now seemed to be causing the entire room to pulsate. And the young girls screamed.

From the audience, someone requested *Great Balls of Fire*.

"Sorry," bragged John, "but my own songs are much better."

"You have the gift, Johnny," came a voice from the corner.

It was his father. Why was he here?

John tried to ignore him, looking instead across the other side of the room. He could see people he knew, although he seemed to have forgotten many of their names.

Except now he noticed that Shelly was in the crowd, not paying any attention to him at all. Finally, she looked his way, but refused to make eye contact and turned away, toward another man . . . a lesser man, really.

And the music turned stale. John's fingers were suddenly tight, his mind fractured.

The crowd sensed his distraction and quickly abandoned him.

"We want a real artist," someone yelled.

"Pretender," scowled another.

John tried to continue playing, but the piano made no sound and the stage was already being dismantled.

The room was now silent.

"Don't mind the piano player," Shelly whispered to her new lover. "He's just an old man who imagines I might somehow love him. He means nothing to me."

This was a glimpse of Shelly that John could not have imagined possible. It couldn't be . . .

"No," he said. "I love you more than anything, forever."

"Forever?" someone blurted from the crowd. "You'll be dead forever."

"And why would I even want him?" Shelly asked the gallery. "Just look at his body."

The crowd laughed and began to leave. As did Shelly, not even bothering to look back, her boyfriend protecting her exit from any competitor. John was left to the taunts of a few, who now seemed to be his closest and only friends.

"She doesn't love you," they said quietly.

"I thought she did," said John. "I thought there was actually a chance."

\*\*\*\*

John was weak, devastated.

Instinctively, he picked up the pen and notebook at the side of his bed. His hand was still asleep, probably from a lack of blood, but he needed to write.

> *A thousand bull rhinos roamed across his body, slashing his heart until there was absolutely nothing left . . . as if it had never even existed.*

Bull rhinos? That sounds ridiculous, he thought. But what could demolish his being with any more pain and finality? How could he accurately describe the anguish he was feeling?

What was he thinking? It was a dream. He knew it was a dream. Shelly would never do that to him. She wouldn't embarrass him. She wouldn't turn against him. It was all in his head. His brain was playing tricks again and he wasn't going to fall for this absurdity.

He just needed to relax, to start thinking clearly. Perhaps there was some new kind of medicine that might somehow help, a cure for being old and in everyone's way. He just needed to get his damn mind under control.

That's what he needed . . .

\*\*\*\*

Daniel's wife knocked, then opened the door.

"John, I just made popcorn," she said. "It's in the living room if you would like some. Or I could bring you a bowl."

John looked at her. What was her name? She lives in this house. She's married to Daniel. He's known her for years. Her name? How could he forget? What was wrong with his brain?

"Yes," he said. "I'll be out in a few minutes. Thank you."

The woman smiled and left.

This was a test, he thought. His mind wasn't *that* deteriorated. Yes, there were lapses, but it would come back. He'd remember. All he had to do was slowly cover the alphabet. If he got the first letter, he'd remember the rest. What was her name? This was so damn frustrating.

John's mind frantically traced each letter. He was up to J. Jessica, Janet, Joan, Jo . . .

Joe Mazelli.

There was a guy named Joe Mazelli who pitched for Lehigh. That had to be 80 years ago. Joe Mazelli was Lehigh's ace, a lefty with a sizzling fastball and a deadly curve. But he threw some fat pitches on that day and John had ripped him for three hits in a game that was played at their field in Bethlehem, Pennsylvania. Two doubles and a homerun to dead center with a stroke so smooth and powerful that John didn't even feel the ball off his bat. God, what a feeling that was.

John knocked in five runs and Bucknell won, 9-4.

Joe Mazelli.

How absurd was this predicament? John had remembered

171

the name of some guy he had played baseball against in 1920 but couldn't recall the name of the woman who was married to his best friend and had made dinner for him not more than two hours ago?

What was her name?

Katherine. Of course, Katherine.

Ever so slowly, John headed for the popcorn.

# CHAPTER 13

Daniel began retrieving John's writings from the garage, a few boxes at a time. Considering John's energy level, it would undoubtedly take him a few months of solid work to get through them all.

"Don't try to rush yourself," Daniel suggested.

"I just want to soak up a few old ideas," John replied. "Maybe see what I've forgotten."

John looked carefully over the outside of the first several boxes Daniel had lugged into his room, searching for a hint of familiarity. One seemed to have *MARY* scribbled on the top, along with several other words, but they had all faded badly.

John opened the box as if probing for some precious treasure. He pulled out an initial pile of papers and notebooks. At first, he found nothing of consequence. In fact, some of the stuff seemed rather scrambled and bland.

But then he came across a large envelope with *Remembering Mary* etched in a bold stroke on the cover. He knew instantly what it contained. Inside were several postcards, along with personal documents and loose pages of diary notes John had written about his sister.

He glanced at a postcard, dated October 25, 1940, with a picture of Paul Revere's grave on the front. You would never guess that this was a woman whose art could crawl into your

173

soul. She certainly couldn't pick out a postcard.

> *Dear Johnny,*
>
> *I'm in love. His name is Peter Orwell. I think you'll be relieved to know he's not an artist or even in the business. But he is wildly handsome. And, best of all, he totally understands me and accepts my artistic moods.*
>
> *I'll see you at Thanksgiving. You promised to come. I can't wait for you to meet him. He's absolutely perfect.*
>
> *– Mary*

Peter Orwell was perfect alright, John thought, as he tried to picture the man who would murder his sister just six months later.

Mary had always been a terrible judge of men.

Here was something John had written five years earlier, dated June 12, 1935:

> *Quite a day. Dad and I committed Mary to a mental hospital. The doctors said it would take at least six months, maybe longer, they didn't know. I feel like a jailer, but there's no choice. She's an absolute mess. It's as if she has lost her mind and has no clue where to find it.*

It seemed that Mary Hammond could never establish proper checkpoints. She was either blissfully happy or tragically depressed. Times of calm and grace were always followed by fear and turmoil.

At the hospital, they gave her clay.

"Safe therapy," the doctor said.

John could only cringe as one of the world's most acclaimed artists just sat and stared, or muttered, or cried, or played with her clay. At times she would run her fingers through its guts as if she sensed her extraordinary talent, or maybe she would just heave it to the floor, a lost art ever dying inside her rage.

Hers was a creativity that channeled directly into madness and destruction. John had not noticed these traits in her childhood and was not sure how the sickness had burrowed into her mind. It must have been slow and cunning.

At the time, John assumed that returning to sanity could be triggered by a slight snap of the brain. He wasn't even close.

Mary fought the insanity for years, most often denying she even had problems. In fact, she frequently boasted that she had regained complete control of her fragile mind; that she had fought and won the brave battle. But the unbalance would always return.

The last time John had seen her, Thanksgiving of 1940, she had seemed so exuberant and happy, almost to a fault. Strange, but John had read her enthusiasm as a bad sign. She may have been in love again, but he knew the emotional high would not last. He knew she would crash, she always did.

John's mind pulled away. Once again, what was the point of pondering about something that no longer existed? She had been his sister, but their lives rarely crossed. He still remembered the moment he learned of her death. His father had sent a telegram; words without adjectives.

*Mary dead. Murdered. Details later.*

What was that all about? Could not he have phoned the

news? Was he that fearful of showing emotion? Whatever, it wasn't worth thinking about what might have been inside his father's mind.

John recalled that his own mind immediately tried to process such a strange event. For a moment, it had seemed impossible that his sister could actually be dead. And why didn't he feel remorse? Mostly, he remembered a certain aggravation that he would probably have to travel to Boston for the funeral, followed by guilt that he could be so callous.

Great artist, pitiful person, a passing that did not linger. In fact, David's death had somehow made more of an impact, probably because of the rat poison, of all things. David Hammond didn't even care to die without pain, opting to tear apart his own guts, to viciously destroy himself, to carry his disdain for life to the ultimate instant.

And there was John's mother in her final days, the incessant cough he wished would be silent, a sound that would not stop pounding on the door to his mind, a deep and wispy gag that was steady and uncontrollable, as if death was sliding down her throat.

Trying to escape the room, John could hear his mother's disgusting noises. He desperately wanted to fall asleep. He just wanted her to stop.

"If you're going to die, just die," he whispered under his covers, then berated himself for having such a horrible thought as to request the death of his own mother. Yes, she was in pain, but he wanted her to get well, to survive. He wanted her to smile and laugh and hold him again. He wanted her to live forever. Saying he hoped she would die just so he could get some sleep? It was easily his worst moment of cruelty.

The cough did eventually subside, but the pneumonia had already taken control and her body could no longer handle the strain.

John wondered if somewhere her spirit had been watching over him all these years, knowing he had once wished her death just to silence an irritating cough.

Or did her soul realize anything at all?

For a moment, his father's death passed through his mind, but just a flicker he quickly shut down, abruptly turning to another corridor.

John realized it was peculiar that he nearly always seemed to remember the members of his family more for the instants of their deaths than the time they were alive.

****

John stuffed Mary's papers back into the envelope. Her murder had been big news throughout the world; it would have been a feast for the tabloids of 1999. But even back then, the gossip surrounding Mary's bizarre death managed to fester.

And, as always, the auction block proved most kind to a dead artist. Those who had purchased Mary Hammond's earlier works immediately tripled their price tag and those who bought from them quickly doubled their investment.

After all, this was true art—rare, original, never again.

****

Halfway into the box, John found an old manuscript. Evidently, it had no title. Of course, now he remembered. This was going to be his mystery novel. He had written a bit over 100 pages about a man trying to solve the murder of his wife, only to uncover secrets about her that he had never suspected. The story would probably be considered tame by today's cultural measurements, but the underlying theme still had relevance—good people hiding scandalous baggage.

> *The shot was a blur, the bullet leaving and entering within an instant, its launch a mere fidget of the finger, one streak through the heart, its penetration pure and final, a thousand screams racing across the silent universe.*
>
> *She fell, lifeless.*
>
> *He stood in shock as the killer escaped to darkness, his mind now jammed into slow motion as his eyes blazed back to his wife. What had just happened? Was this a mistake?*
>
> *He looked down at her, horrified as others pulled him back, crowding the space while tearing him away from his love. And there was panic and shouting and a quiet hopelessness. He saw no angels, no ghosts, just death.*

John stopped reading, his mind suddenly energized. With the right actors and a hot soundtrack, this would make a great movie.

Then again, it was just another work he would never complete.

He moved on, looking for substance.

****

John's mind was busy.

This entire exercise was stupid. *The Brave Historian* cannot be some odd puzzle that's stuck together with pieces of his other writings. It would be better to gather his best works and present them precisely as they existed. So what if some of them were not finished?

Life is never complete, John told himself, there's always something that's left undone. Would it be possible for a person to catalog everything they had ever read or seen or done? Of course not. In fact, everything to do with living is eventually left behind.

Mary, David, his father; none of them had finished creating. There could have been more.

Actually, the family made quite a bit of money selling the fragments of Mary's creations. She had hundreds of incomplete projects. David led the plundering. But three years later, all he would leave behind would be his famous *Death Be but a Short Vacation*, boasting on Page 16 that he had purposely burned all remnants of unpublished works so no one would profit from his brilliance.

In that regard, perhaps that's what John should do—light a match to Daniel's garage and burn it all, everything he had ever written destroyed and forgotten. Except John was not like his brother. And he had no intention of burning down Daniel's garage. Too much could go wrong.

Anyway, it had already been done. And John refused to be remembered as his brother's copycat, if he were to be remembered at all.

It occurred to John that Franz Kafka must certainly have pondered similar questions in his final days of life. As John recalled the story, a 39-year-old Kafka, dying from tuberculosis and once again doubting his own genius, had requested of a friend that, upon death, all of his writings be destroyed. To Kafka's ravaged mind, his writings were incomplete, unknown, worthless, the incessant work of a failure erased by fire.

But the friend was also Kafka's editor and no way could

he burn such brilliant words and thoughts, no matter how scattered the organization.

Now, of course, Kafka is considered one of the great writers of the 20th century.

John lobbied his mind in another direction. Perhaps *The Brave Historian* didn't even need Robert Patterson. John could just edit his own writings and present them to the world, his best works in one pile.

And leave a simple note:

> *This is what I did, sorry I didn't finish . . . hope you like it.*

# CHAPTER 14

Wednesday, December 22, 1999 . . . finally.

John painstakingly checked his wardrobe. He wanted to look good today, to be smooth and stylish. Quite frankly, his clothes sucked.

The phone rang. His first thought was that it might be Shelly calling to cancel, still caught in Los Angeles, too much work, something better popped up.

Good, it was some woman inviting him to a time-share presentation for condos in Sedona, Arizona.

"I'm 99 years old," John told her. "It wouldn't be the wisest of investments."

"But it would be a wonderful gift for your family," she interjected with cue No. 47 from her script on how to sell anything to anybody.

"You do like the sunshine?" she added.

"I love the sunshine," he answered. "That's one reason I live in California. And the other reason I live here is because I'm too old to move."

She gave a half-hearted, stupid laugh, undoubtedly to trick her customer into thinking that she thought he was very funny and clever, the kind of man who should buy a time-share.

He wasn't fooled.

She headed for another angle.

181

"These are very comfortable and age-friendly," she said.

"I do like comfort," he answered. "In fact, it's time for my nap."

John had hoped the time-share lady would ultimately offer to conclude the conversation, but soon realized she was one of those pit bull people who never let go, hoping you will crumble from the pain and agree to buy anything just to get them off the line. He had no choice but to hang up the phone.

Needing to refocus, he looked at the mirror. Still the same old man, dressed like it was 1943.

****

There had been that other woman while Shelly was gone, the one in the dream.

John still had a taste, but he could no longer picture her. He wished the unknown woman had been Shelly and that led him down yet another brief and wild avenue of his mind.

****

Shelly arrived early, actually giving John a hug. John noted her warm cheek, embrace and that crazy scent of perfume. Yes, he was willing to consider permanent residence, but she pulled away, her smile so lovely and honest. He also realized she had put her hand softly to his back, either the sign of a deeper connection or she just didn't want him to fall, probably the latter.

"Let's talk again about the art of writing," she said.

No, that was not what he wanted to talk about. He had envisioned something more personal.

"Haven't we already covered that?"

"Slightly," she said, "but I want to discuss the creativity that goes into writing."

"Okay," he sighed. "there are more interesting subjects, you know."

"I know," she giggled.

Hmmm, he thought.

"You had mentioned the characters in your story become like old friends," Shelly continued. "Let's talk about that."

"Well, it is definitely a stimulating aspect of writing," he said. "You create characters for a story and you really know nothing about them. Sometimes they don't click, but you keep at it. Eventually, you find yourself thinking about them all the time, as if they exist. You give them personality, purpose, and they take residence within your mind. You try to figure out how they might think or act or where the plot might lead them, continually opening a seam in your own imagination. And ever so slowly, they start becoming real people, as if you know them, as if they are friends or enemies. You love them, despise them and, in your mind, it often seems as if they have taken over the writing. 'No, I wouldn't do that,' they'll argue. 'This is what I would do and why I would do it.' And they only need you to scribble down their words or thoughts. It's strange and crazy, but that's what happens."

Jeremy Mueller had been that way, taking residence within John's mind during the five years he was writing *The Man with Total Control*. It had been a slow start, but *The Brave Historian*, Robert Patterson, had now secured the role of John's imaginary best friend.

"Behind the walls of his existence," John quipped to Shelly's camera, "Jeremy Mueller, *The Man with Total Control*, is obsessed with mortality, yet afraid to experience life. On the other hand, Robert Patterson, *The Brave Historian*, wants to encounter life's great adventures, although something is always holding him back, as if imprisoned by the very barriers he seeks to shed. Both men are complicated and fragile."

John looked away from the camera and directly at Shelly, as if she already knew the two characters of his mind and pen.

"It's funny, Daniel or Katherine will say something to me, and I am totally tuned out. I mean, these are real people, an important part of my life, but I can't pay attention to whatever they are talking about because I've got an entirely different conversation happening inside my brain with a bunch of fictional characters. And they always take precedence. It's quite rude, but I can't help it, the people I make up are incredibly demanding."

John laughed at the conundrum.

"Of course," he continued, "if I were a character in a book, I'm certain I'd be that way, totally demanding. In fact, the way my brain operates, I'd probably drive the poor writer nuts."

Shelly could not help but join John's conversation.

"John, let's face it," she said. "Any writer who would have created you is already past crazy."

John laughed at her insight, secretly wishing she hadn't been so perceptive, because now he loved her even more.

"I would guess," said Shelly, "that all serious writers are possessed by the characters they have created. At times, maybe all authors have difficulty distinguishing between real and imagined."

"But it's not like I'm delusional," said John. "I don't see ghosts or shadows. I don't talk out loud to Jeremy Mueller or Robert Patterson or The Magician, or the hundreds of other characters swarming around in there. To the real world, I keep every one of them silent."

John paused, wondering if his thoughts needed any further explanation. He grinned.

"I do have to slow down at times and take a few deep breaths to remind myself of reality," he said. "Otherwise, it gets exceedingly busy inside my head."

"John, you had told me several weeks ago that you had written about a dozen books, all in various stages of completion. What did you mean by that?"

"Well, just that they're all sort of done, but not quite," he said. "They just need some minor touch-ups, just a few more drafts."

"But, you've never had any of your books published?" she said, having already asked that question in an earlier interview.

"No," he said with a touch of agitation, "they just never seem to be completely done."

"Why?"

"I don't know. I've thought about it for years. My guess is that I'm anchored by this notion that the book has to be better than anything before it. So, I go over and over the same stories, continually changing a word or idea, fiddling with content as if it's an obsession. Believe me, the stories do get better."

"But never done," she inserted.

"Maybe if I were only 70 again, maybe then."

John stopped, gesturing with his face and hands that whatever he was talking about didn't really matter.

"To be honest," he continued, "it has only become more and more difficult to fool myself. I'm too old. The only thing finished is my energy."

Shelly's urge was to disagree, to comfort, to tell John he had plenty of good years left, but why deny the obvious.

"Has anyone ever read your books?"

"No, well, Daniel has seen a few of my things, but not much."

"But, you would still like for them to be published, wouldn't you?"

"Sure, I've always wanted to be a famous writer, if not a piano player or, better yet, a baseball star. I don't think I'm that much different from most people in that I've always had this desire to be center stage. I guess I'm just hesitant to get up there, or maybe even a bit afraid."

"Why would you be afraid?" she asked, suddenly feeling like some world-renowned psychologist carefully mending the mental barriers of another failed genius.

"I don't think I could stand the criticism, so I avoid the risk," he said. "All things considered, it seems to be easier not to try. And I don't know why that is. It's all very senseless, but I can't seem to shake it. Now, if I were coaching a baseball team, I'd tell my players just the opposite, give them one of those 'go for it and never give up' motivational speeches. I know the cliché, the biggest failure is to have never tried, I know."

Shelly took a deep breath. Another time, this might be a fascinating discussion, but not now. There was something else she had to ask, but had held off for the right moment with no plan of when to strike.

Go ahead, she thought, just blurt it out.

"John, what happened to your daughter?"

\*\*\*\*

And John's mind plunged into slow motion . . .

There was a time he had thought it beautiful, this majestic mountain on the banks of the Susquehanna River, just across from the small, central Pennsylvania borough of Northumberland, where two of the river's strongest branches veer sharply into one another, heading south with an ultimate destination to the Chesapeake Bay.

But the cliff itself was dangerous, a sheer drop of more than 500 feet; not to water, but straight to dirt and rock.

John's thoughts accelerated.

Had Sarah even realized what was happening? They said the old man never did let go of her, squeezed her firmly into his own death, as if protecting her.

John remembered the coroner and police quietly discussing velocity and the impossibility of survival. They had assumed that John's mind was too deep in shock to possibly be listening, but his was a stunned focus busily gathering the most minor of details he would certainly never forget; like the sudden coolness in the air, a small bird flying past with such ease, the look of horror and empathy on the face of the one policeman who surely had children of his own . . .

"It could have been an accident," they would say, but the footprints at the top of the cliff suggested otherwise.

Looking back, John should have been more aware. His father had been sick for months. His mind had been terribly distracted, his color ghostly, his only pleasure seeming to be the time with his grandchild. John and Jessica had been thrilled the old man could care so much for her. It was good for his spirits, they agreed. And it would someday give their daughter wonderful memories of her grandfather.

But there would be no memories for Sarah.

John pictured her beautiful smile and, just for a moment, he felt great comfort. But then hopelessness triggered anger and the hollow despair took hold, as it always did.

John pulled away, trying to move back in time, to somehow stop that one awful evening in the early spring of 1950. "No, Dad, we don't need a baby-sitter today. We're staying home. Sarah will be with us. You go on alone."

That was all he would have had to say.

John's mind stood behind them now, looking over the shoulders of his father and daughter, looking down the cliff. He had seen this before, both in dreams and awake. As always, he could not stop them.

Ever silent, George Hammond picked up the little girl, hugged her tight in his arms and slowly walked off the edge.

\*\*\*\*

John stared at Shelly and didn't back down. Past the beauty, he realized her compassion. He felt safe with her. It was time to let go the hidden truth that had haunted him for years.

"My father killed my daughter," he said abruptly. "He was sick, near death, and I guess he was too frightened to die alone."

John stopped, trying to deceive a heart long wrecked by age and circumstance.

"I shouldn't talk about this," he said. "I have never spoken about what happened. I just wanted to forget, longing that it would go away or that somehow life would turn around and I could save her and hold her and keep her forever."

His breath was slow, shaky. His hands were busy, tense. His eyes tried desperately to block the tears waiting cautiously to escape.

John tried to wipe them away, but more followed.

"The police said it was not an accident, that he held my little girl and jumped off a cliff. And they kept saying how strange it was that he never let go of her, never let go."

Again John turned silent.

"How old was Sarah?" asked Shelly, struggling to keep her voice and heart from collapsing.

"Only two years old," he said, looking down as to somehow control his long-broken emotions.

"Tell me about her."

"She was beautiful, a lot like her mother. But we always

agreed and laughed that she had my personality. She was a thinker, creative, so much fun. I believe she would have been an artist of some kind."

"You must have been devastated," said Shelly.

"I was weak, numb. In an instant, life had turned from wonderful to horrendous. I couldn't get her out of my mind, but I also couldn't get her back. What destroyed me the most was the reality of what she would never be . . . so brutally unfair. All that was left was to hate my father and yearn for my baby.

"I did a lot of pretending. Once I even pictured her sitting on God's knee and talking about how she couldn't wait to see her daddy again and wondering if I would bring her a present; as if she still existed, as if there was a God, as if history would suddenly change and she'd come back . . . if just for a moment.

"I became a tragic figure, unable to even think about coping with the world. Eventually I returned to work, but people kept their distance."

Shelly was lost. She wanted to tell John that, really, there was a Heaven, that Sarah was with God, knowing that she would see him again, this time forever. Maybe Shelly could ease John's mind, to bring hope and truth. She stayed silent.

"Time and again," he continued, "I still think of her and it hurts. She'd be 52 years old, probably happily married with three or four kids and a successful career. She might even be a grandmother. Sometimes I think these things are actually happening in another dimension; just out of touch, maybe a place by the ocean or in the mountains, yet somewhere we can't really see, or visit . . . sorry, my mind takes crazy paths."

Shelly could see John was drained, but knew he wanted to continue.

"What about your wife, Jessica. What happened to her?"

"Jessica was distraught after Sarah died. We both were.

I think we hoped our love would be strong enough to pull us through. We held each other and cried, but we could barely talk. We couldn't even look into each other's eyes. It was as if we were lost in different directions. The silence went on for what seemed like forever. Time just didn't want to move and Jessica couldn't stand the pain. When it finally became too much, she turned away. She went to find Sarah, to follow her down."

"Follow her down?" repeated Shelly, not sure what he meant.

"It was January of 1951, bitterly cold with wind chills that went way below zero. I remember at the newspaper, we were talking about how the snows had become coated in ice and the clouds had hidden the sun for more than a week. It was also exactly nine months since Sarah had died."

John tried to take a long breath, his eyes distant, his voice dry.

"Jessica made her way to the same cliff and took the same last step. I can only suppose she was thinking that maybe this would be the path to find our baby, to be united in death. You might say that, in some respect, she did the same thing as my father. And I've often wondered if maybe they were right. Perhaps the three of them are sitting around eternity at this very moment having a great time, wondering what's taking me so damn long to get there."

"You never considered jumping from that cliff?" asked Shelly, immediately shocked at the thought she would pose such a question.

"Not lately," he said. "Pennsylvania is three thousand miles to the east and I doubt I will ever be there again. But it is an interesting theory Jessica tested; that you might be able to join someone by dying in the same manner. Then again, that hardly seems logical or scientifically possible."

Again, Shelly had the urge to share her faith.

John closed his eyes, rubbing his fingers hard across his forehead. His body slumped forward, suddenly weary. He continued to speak.

"They say that eventually the wounds will disappear, with time there is distance. But that's total bullshit. Maybe you forget every now and then, but distance never heals the scars, never."

# CHAPTER 15

It was already the day after Christmas and Shelly needed to seriously start working on the new millennium segment for Channel 5. She had told the station manager it would take her only a few hours to put the thing together, a painful miscalculation on her part. It had already been more than a week. She had to admit she was facing major problems.

This should be easy, she thought. It's only a three-minute piece. I've done this kind of thing before. But not like this. It had to be perfect, a prize-winning short documentary on the life of John Hammond. Unfortunately, she wasn't at all happy with what she had put together.

The people in L.A. moved quickly — they made decisions and forged ahead to the next project. Yet she seemed stalled over an otherwise simple chore. Bob Beatty would be calling from Channel 5 and he would wonder what was taking her so long with this minor assignment. Or maybe he had forgotten and she'd be totally off the hook. Even so, she needed to think of an excuse in case he did phone. Okay, she'd had a bad case of the flu and she was just too sick to do any work. No, she was too much of a hypochondriac. Even pretending to have been sick might result in her actually coming down with some horrible disease and ultimately dying because of a stupid lie.

Okay, she had taken on a huge assignment for a Fortune

500 company, was saddled with an inflexible deadline, and someone had stolen the film from her car. Right, make it lame.

Forget the excuses, she finally told herself, just do the work. Don't worry about it being completely flawless. Besides, this piece is really just a starting point for John Hammond's story. It's only a first draft for something much deeper. Why waste a great story for three minutes on local news? She didn't have to include his entire biography. All she really needed was the bit about John turning 100 and living in three centuries and being the last of the Hammonds. Sure, she should include his great undiscovered talents. She could easily throw that together. A few edits and she could have the whole thing ready within an hour.

No, she couldn't.

Who was she kidding? She wasn't a newscaster, particularly of the Hollywood variety. She wasn't that refined. She wasn't that shallow. She didn't have the voice, the diction, the smooth delivery, the grooming, the finely chiseled features, or the journalistic presence. She didn't have any of those things. Those people all came from the same school of broadcasting. They had the same Action News Team finesse. They had that major network style.

Plus, the camera made her look chubby.

Hold it, she thought. This isn't about me; it's about John Hammond. Just be creative, give it a shot, see where it goes and don't worry about failure. If Channel 5 doesn't like it, they just won't run it. She could handle rejection. Lord knows, her ego had taken plenty of poundings.

Don't even consider negative thoughts. All she had to do was gather the various pieces of film — a couple of John's best comments, a few scrapbook shots for a taste of his youth, some pictures of his famous family, him playing the piano and reading some of what he's written. She had plenty. Just splice it together and then write a script.

Besides, this was precisely what she wanted to do with her life. This was her career path. Big deal if she wasn't a member of the Action News Team.

She had the plan. It didn't have to be great. Just put together a three-minute video and try to look skinny.

\*\*\*\*

John was trying to remember when Shelly said she would return. It had only been several days since he'd last seen her, but he had no idea if she had mentioned anything about returning.

Maybe she didn't; maybe it was over, and he'd never see her again.

No, she always made another appointment. She would definitely come back, or at least call. Still, the uncertainty was troubling.

Suddenly, he felt a strong, sharp pain in the center of his heart. This can't be . . .

His mind turned immediately to the problem. It's just a pain, he told himself, a common pain.

John hastily picked up his notebook, his mind monitoring all movement. He tried to write quickly, to somehow pull his brain into a new activity. His words were shaky:

> *The snake has struck and there is no escape. The body tenses into shock as the venom spreads, the mind giving garbled orders to stay calm.*
>
> *In shock, the brain attempts to wrestle itself from the stricken body, momentarily fooling itself into*

*thinking it might have a chance to break away, to explore the universe under its own power.*

*But hope turns futile as all thought crumbles. Dying within the ruins of yet another stunned mind, one helpless fragment of awareness screams, angry that the body could be so selfish.*

John needed to walk, to get away from this nonsense.

He tried to stand, but moved too quickly and was now suddenly dizzy, the room swirling in a jittery procession. He needed to sit back down; slowly, relax. Perhaps it's just indigestion. Yes, he had just eaten some grapes. That had to be the problem. Forget that his head was feeling light, he just needed to breathe deep and calm. Don't think about death, just breathe.

Finally, the pain subsided. He felt much better. He needed to write.

*On the verge of defeat, I find myself standing guard against the skies. There is no need to seek help. One thing about death is that very few people notice . . .*

**\*\*\*\***

Shelly's mind was motoring into high gear.

"Perfect," she said to herself while again reviewing her three-minute and one-second masterpiece on John Hammond. What had she been worrying about? This was a wonderful story and she captured it all; certainly enough to impress the folks at Channel 5.

This was good stuff. She was pumped.

\*\*\*\*

Daniel had brought two more cardboard boxes to John's room.

"If you need any help, just yell," he said.

"Wait," said John, hesitating to corral Daniel's full attention. "Do you know if the girl who's doing the film mentioned when she was coming back?"

"Tuesday afternoon," said Daniel. "Day after tomorrow, don't you remember? You were the one who told me yesterday that Shelly was going to be back on December 28th."

"Sorry, my mind is a blank today," said John, "but it's good she's coming. It's good."

Daniel stood at the door.

"You sort of like her, don't you," he said.

"As a friend," John quickly shot back.

"I don't know about that," laughed Daniel. "I think you've got the hots for her."

"The hots?" grumbled John, trying to act disinterested. "People my age don't get the hots."

"But, you are blushing," Daniel joked, a devious smile plastered across his face. "Plus, that baloney you just tossed my way about 'the girl who's doing the film.' You know her name."

"Okay, she's good looking," admitted John. "You got me. What can I say? I can dream."

"Me too," said Daniel. "But don't tell Katherine."

Daniel continued the smile as he turned to leave.

"Yep, we can both dream," he mumbled, adding an overacted sigh.

John was stunned. What did that mean? Did Daniel also

have feelings for Shelly? Maybe he was just kidding. He's married. John had not even considered this irritating possibility, the rush of jealousy beginning its unfair attack. Daniel was plotting to steal Shelly's love.

John had no defense. Shelly didn't even know he was the one who truly loved her; that his passion was desperate and wild, and hopeless.

Then again, he probably didn't need to worry about Daniel's rivalry. To Shelly, they were both old men.

\*\*\*\*

John had joined Daniel and Katherine to watch a four-hour CBS special counting down the Top 100 stories of the 20th century. The kids buzzed in and out of the room, totally disinterested.

John winced as they reached No. 77, the rise of the interstate highway system.

"That's a joke," he exclaimed, pointing his finger at the TV screen. "Who made up this stupid list? Interstate highways totally changed America. Number seventy-seven? Don't get me started."

"It's just a list, John," said Daniel. "I just want to see where they rank the Beatles."

"Yes, that will be exciting," said John. "Meanwhile, I'm going to take a nap. Wake me up when they get to the top ten."

In his room, John listened to a CD of old Johnny Mathis hits; *Chances Are, The Twelfth of Never, Wild Is the Wind*, and fell into a deep sleep.

\*\*\*\*

He saw it prowling, on the hill behind the trees, huge eyes fixed on its prey . . . staring at him.

At first, John had a hard time realizing exactly what he was seeing. But, yes, it definitely was a lion, its body thick with power and grace, and death.

John was fortunate to be sitting inside his car, behind the wheel with the keys safely inside the ignition switch, ready to drive away in an instant.

The lion moved closer.

John was food to him, nothing more. But surely the beast must realize that John had a mind, that he was special.

The lion had now left the trees. It seemed amazing to John that such a large animal could move so gently. He had a dignity worthy of respect, but his presence was alarming.

Lucky I'm safe, thought John, lucky I'm protected.

The lion was now at the rear window on the passenger side of the car, his eyes focused on John's body. Still, the window was closed, so there was no problem that this beast was peering at John from only a few feet away. Except the other window, on the front passenger side, was rolled completely down. John had not realized it until that very moment. Maybe the lion would not notice, would just go away.

But the lion does notice, and now is staring from inside the front window; his hot, stale breath filling the vacuum of an area that once seemed impenetrable . . . and John suddenly realizes there is no protection.

Wait, thinks John, I can still leave. I just need to start the car. But I dare not take my eyes off the killer. Start the car, stupid.

John tried to move, but the lion's gigantic claw had reached through the open window and trapped both of his hands. At first, it was soft, but now the power and pressure were terribly painful. John could not move. And still the lion stared, eyes in command, his claws trapping, penetrating, ripping the door from its hinges.

John struggled to break free, one hand pulling away, until the lion's other paw pounded down to lock it as well. Still, the eyes . . .

No longer caring to play, the lion ripped its claw through the chest, leaving John to watch his own death, a ravaged body silently pulsing in shock. So easy, so swift, so total.

I should have rolled up the window, thought John.

\*\*\*\*

The room was dark, the day gone. John's mind twitched, his body barely able to move. His hand moved quickly to his chest, feeling for life. Good, no blood.

In the distance, he could hear the muffled chatter of the television.

\*\*\*\*

Zack answered the door. It was a woman.

"Hi, you must be Zack," she said. "I'm Shelly Kingston. I've been filming a documentary about John. Is John or your dad home?"

"Sure, come in," said Zack, impressed that this woman actually made movies.

Daniel was surprised to see Shelly, as was his wife. Katherine had not paid much attention to whom was doing the filming of John's story. This woman was quite young and attractive.

Katherine glanced at Daniel, whose face was slightly blushed. She sensed an unsteady pause in his demeanor, causing an alarm to resonate in her seldom-used radar of wifely concern.

"Shelly," said Daniel, trying desperately, for no apparent reason, to seem casual. "I didn't realize you were coming over tonight."

"Well, I wasn't," she said. "I was in the area and I have a piece of film I wanted to show to you and John."

"Zack, why don't you go tell John we have a guest," said Daniel, his eyes never leaving Shelly. "Sorry for the mess. We were just watching TV. Oh, I'm sorry, Shelly Kingston, this is my wife, Katherine."

Both Katherine and Shelly took one step forward.

"Nice to meet you," said Katherine.

"You too, Katherine. John has mentioned you several times in our interviews. It's a pleasure to finally meet you."

Meanwhile, John couldn't get down the hall fast enough. Was Zack pulling a prank? Did Daniel put him up to it? He had no idea Shelly was coming tonight. He didn't look too good, but hopefully she wouldn't notice. He had to be careful not to stumble or lose his breath. Take your time, he tried to tell himself.

"Hi Shelly," he said as he limped into the room, rather winded. "I didn't realize you were coming over tonight. But, don't get me wrong, it's great you are here."

Did he seem a bit too excited?

"Thanks John," she said in that beautiful voice. "I just came by for a few minutes, so I hope I didn't disturb anyone."

"No," both John and Daniel said at the same time.

Katherine was still focused on Daniel's reactions to the visitor.

"Well," said Shelly. "Like I mentioned the other day, Channel 5, the station in Los Angeles, wants to air a short piece about John for their evening news. Anyway, I've put together three minutes of video that I'm going to send up to them and I think they're going to run it within the next few days. Actually, nothing is certain in this business. But I think they are really going to like it. So, I thought I'd stop by and premiere it for you guys."

"Great," said Daniel.

"Yikes," added John. "I don't know if I want to watch this or not."

"Just pretend you're watching someone else," said Shelly, suddenly feeling somewhat nervous. She needed their opinion to be positive.

"It's just a first effort," she said in slight fabrication. Truthfully, she had done about 15 drafts, but they didn't need to know.

"I wasn't sure if you had a DVD player, so I brought a tape and disc."

"See Katherine," laughed Daniel, nodding toward his wife. "I told you we need one of those DVD players."

Momentarily, Daniel wondered why his wife looked so uncomfortable.

"Just remember," said Shelly, "I can still make changes."

Daniel ignored his wife's weird look and popped Shelly's tape into the VCR. Ashley and Zack quickly battled for the best chair.

"Fasten your seat belts," mumbled John as Daniel hit the *PLAY* button.

\*\*\*\*

Shelly was first on the screen, portraying perfectly a well-schooled and beautiful newscaster.

"Just before midnight on New Year's Eve," she said to the camera, "John Garfield Hammond will turn 100 years old. And as the world celebrates the new millennium, he will gracefully step into his third century on earth."

Well, didn't take her long to reveal the gimmick, thought John. Three centuries on earth; please, hold your applause.

The old man felt rather odd watching his family photographs flash across the TV screen. There he was as a child in Pennsylvania, that photo of him playing college baseball, and now the lines of his ancient face peering way too close to the camera.

"I remember telling my younger brother I was going to live 100 years," John was saying.

Far beyond any original expectations, the video was quite good.

Excellent job, thought Daniel. Shelly is a total fox.

I look so damn old, thought John.

Shelly was now mentioning the three legends of the Hammond Family. And there was John talking about writing, his wife and daughter, and now he was playing the piano.

John was beginning to feel dizzy. Why did she use the piano segment? Finally, it was over.

"For John Hammond, it has been an amazing journey," Shelly was saying as the camera turned its focus toward her.

She paused.

"This is Shelly Kingston reporting from Escondido in North San Diego County."

\*\*\*\*

"Amazing," said Daniel as everyone but John began applauding. "I'd say it's great. And that was a real nice touch with my buddy, John, playing the piano."

"Two thumbs up," beamed Zack as Ashley followed his gesture.

"Thanks everyone," said Shelly. "It's tough to cram John's

life into three minutes. That's a lot of years."

Oops, maybe she shouldn't have said that.

"Try living those 100 years," joked John.

Shelly was relieved he didn't take her stupid comment as an insult.

"Well, what do you think?" she asked John.

"I thought it was great," he said. "The only change I might suggest is that you hire an actor to play my role, maybe Robert Redford."

"Sorry," kidded Shelly, "I think you're perfect for the lead character."

"But Redford definitely looks better on camera," said John, still trying to make fun of how hideous his face had somehow become.

"You know, John," said Shelly, turning serious, "some people can see beauty in the heart and soul of a person. When I look at you, I really don't see the lines on your face."

She stopped.

John couldn't help but stare, his mouth slightly open. She had caught him totally off guard. He wanted her to continue with what she was saying. What exactly did she mean? Was she really telling the truth? Could it be she was trying to relay a hidden message that she had feelings for him?

"You're too kind," he said.

Damn, he didn't want to say it that way. He wanted to say he deeply loved her and now he realized she loved him, and would she stay the night? Just one night, this night.

****

It was late, the house quiet with sleep, except for John.

He figured Shelly was probably home by now, in her bed . . .

Had she actually made a pass at him? Or had his imagination taken an innocent thought and crudely turned it into a romantic advance? He should just ignore it, forget what she said or how she said it or what she may have meant.

Or, better yet, he should just take the chance and tell her exactly what he was thinking. At the very worst, it might bother her that he would think such a thing, that he wanted to make love with her.

He stopped, trying to process her reaction.

"You want to sleep with me?" she would probably say. "John, I thought we were friends. You could be my great grandfather. You're an old man."

Still, there was no old man in John's mind, just a young boy, and he was aroused.

Besides, if she did push him away and call him a dirty and stupid old man, he could just plead that his mind had played a momentary trick on him and he didn't realize what he was doing, and he would never try to offend her or harm their friendship. She would certainly understand and forgive him. It was all a mistake. He was old and distracted. She'd probably blame herself.

Or maybe that wouldn't happen at all. Maybe she would respond, hold him tightly, passionately . . .

Enough, it was time to act. He was going to ask her. She could scorn him, even laugh. He had nothing to lose but his own pointless dignity.

It was settled.

In the middle of the night, John thought carefully about how he should approach her. He had to be precise and not back down. He would definitely make the move. He would do it the next time they were alone. And he didn't need to rehearse. He would speak from the heart.

\*\*\*\*

In the dim light of shadowed darkness, John could see the naked figure of a woman standing beside his bed. She said nothing, but he could clearly hear the intense noise of excitement, her body giving definition and sound to the night.

Her legs were lean and strong, her breasts full and seductive, the perspiration on her smooth stomach ravaged the ache within him. Without hesitation, he pulled her to him.

She was soft, firm, and familiar.

He had surely been here before with this same woman. Their bodies seemed to fit together so perfectly.

"John," she whispered, "make love with me once again, just me alone."

Jessica?

His body stopped, but hers kept maneuvering ever closer, ever warmer . . . still alluring, still exciting.

"Jessica, is it you?"

"Of course it is," she laughed. "Who else would it be?"

She was right. Who else could there ever be? She was the one he had vowed to love forever. He held her tighter, aware that he had suddenly recovered the ultimate treasure of his life.

"I love you so much," he said. "Don't ever leave me."

"No one can make that promise," she said while swiftly pushing him away. "You should know that."

She left the bed, her beautiful body still glistening in the dim light, for a moment, anyway, and then she began to fade.

"Jessica, come back," he pleaded. "We need to be together, to be in love."

John woke, desperately feeling his bed for another life. Nothing.

# CHAPTER 16

Shelly was silently scolding herself. She had spent two weeks in L.A. and not even looked at a man. Romance? If someone with any kind of possibility had even caught a glimpse of her, she had not noticed.

Even so, it had become an old story. Late at night and lonely, she would sometimes envision the man she would fall in love with—dark eyes, passionate, intelligent and understanding.

It wasn't that she hadn't experienced a few relationships, but men found her difficult. She was creative, impulsive and always working. She was both tough and fragile. A person would have to appreciate that side of her. It would take a special kind of man to ever truly love her and, of course, for her to love him.

To this point in her life, love had been only momentary, eventually a disaster.

Shelly figured her parents were undoubtedly experiencing a twinge of concern that their only child would never marry and never have children, but she was too immersed in her work to harbor guilt. One day she would meet the perfect man and they would love one another forever. That's just the way it would be.

\* \* \* \*

Anxious about the video, Shelly telephoned Bob Beatty at

Channel 5. The receptionist said he was on another line and would probably be just a second. As she waited, Shelly figured he would say it was about time she called, that he had been concerned about her completing the project, but the piece was brilliant, far beyond what he had envisioned.

"Shelly, how's it going?"

"Fine, Bob, I just called to see if you had received the tape I sent to you of John Hammond?"

There was a pause.

"Oh, yes, I did," he said.

Another pause.

"I apologize because I haven't had time to look at it yet," he continued. "You've caught me between meetings. I'll get to it as soon as possible."

"When do you think it might run?" she asked.

But now she sensed another hesitancy.

"I really don't know," he said. "I'll have to get back to you. I'll give you a call or send an email as soon as I know something. But, thanks for getting this to me. Sorry I can't talk longer, but I've gotta go. Talk to you later."

And that was it.

Not exactly the conversation she had expected, but he was probably just busy. He'd surely like it, she told herself. He had to.

\* \* \* \*

John was resting, his mind busily exploring possibilities.

It would certainly happen quickly, he figured, probably with great force. Within hours after the three-minute news feature was televised in Los Angeles, it would be picked up by the national news.

"Boom," he said to himself.

John took a deep breath and let his rich imagination picture the wild mix of events that would undoubtedly unfold.

The phone would ring nonstop from early morning until late at night. His computer would become loaded with messages from around the globe. Everyone would want a piece of the action. Most obvious would be the media shower from newspapers, radio and television. There'd be columnists, reporters, anchors, network stars. There might even be a couple of sportswriters looking for a fresh angle to their end-of-the-century wrap-up stories. They would all be hungry for quality millennium features.

John momentarily paused, a vague recollection that he might have already explored such crazy ideas, but he could not remember when.

He slid comfortably back to fantasy.

John's story would certainly become a ratings giant, cutting sharply across all demographic pockets. Producers from late night shows, morning talk shows, TV news magazines. Can we visit you? Can you travel to New York, Chicago, Los Angeles? All of them had to have immediate answers.

Sitting back in his chair, John stretched his shoulders and hands. He needed to be prepared.

There would be lawyers and accountants and agents with a stream of big ideas. One guy in John's mind boasted that he had a gigantic deal in the works for a vitamin supplement or nutritional drink or both. Another guy had an idea for a TV movie, but would need just a little start-up money.

John would be careful to investigate every offer. It would be difficult to weed out the con artists, but John would not be fooled, unless by his own brain, now operating in overdrive.

The owner of a reputable auction house in New York City

would want to put together "The Hammond Family Auction." He would arrive in Escondido early the next morning.

Plus, there'd be numerous book possibilities; a string of calls from publishers and literary agents, all of them anxious to see a sample of his writing.

Easy money, fame and glory—sign here, now.

John's mind had somehow turned from possibility to fact, now telling the story in the past tense.

And the amount of mail was absurd, his imagination remembered. A few people sent money, for some odd reason. Hundreds of women—and one man—proposed marriage. And, yes, there was also a death threat.

*You can kiss off reaching 100 because it will never happen, you fucking old peace of shit.*

Peace of shit? The idiot couldn't even spell.

The local police said the letter was undoubtedly a hoax, but it was a federal offence to send such threats through the mail, so the FBI arrived as the auctioneer was leaving. Turns out the FBI had a specialist who would run some lab tests and keep in touch. Please call if you notice anything out of the ordinary.

Out of the ordinary?

This was all in John's imagination, for heaven's sake.

But still the house was surrounded by cameras, reporters and curious fans.

Daniel rushed into the room.

"We need to huddle," he gasped, seemingly near panic. "This is totally out of control."

"You're right," said John. "What are all those people doing in front of the house? They're blocking the street. Isn't there a right to privacy or, at the very least, some sort of vagrancy law?

We need a police escort just to get through the front gate."

"A lot of these offers are great," said Daniel, "but I'm beginning to worry about our safety. The kids can't even go outside to play. Believe me, Katherine is not happy."

"I called Shelly and she'll be here in a couple of minutes," said John.

"Sure," said Daniel, "that's all right with me. We just need a plan on how to handle all of this. It really has become way too bizarre."

Shelly arrived right on time, having battled through the jealous corps of newscasters and their cameras. Why does she get to walk right in, they thought? Who the hell is she?

"Don't even turn on your camera today," John said to Shelly. "The three of us need to talk."

Shelly understood the concern and half expected to be blamed.

"You know, we really should be pleased," said Daniel. "We are receiving a ton of wonderful proposals. A week ago, we would have had no hope of even speaking to these people. And now they're begging for John's time. The ramifications of where this might lead are unbelievable. But, before we get drowned in all of this or John drops over from exhaustion, we need to decide on some rules for being selective. And, most of all, how do we get the crowd outside to leave us alone."

John's nerves were starting to shake. He was beginning to feel as if his body had jumped the track at 200 miles an hour, momentarily airborne, yet certain to crash . . .

Wait, none of this was even real. It hadn't even happened. He was only imagining this stuff. Just relax, breathe deep, get the mind under control, slow down . . .

John pulled back to reality. Geez, he can't even think about things without nearly killing himself.

# THE BRAVE HISTORIAN

* * * *

But, anyway, it really didn't matter what scenarios were brewing inside John's abundantly active brain. All of them would end with a message on Shelly's computer.

She had considered once again trying to call Bob Beatty to see what he thought of the video, but then she saw the email on her screen from RBEATTY. Feeling a surge of excitement, she clicked on the message.

> *Dec. 29, 1999 – 2:43 p.m.*
> *Shelly,*
>    *Nice work on the 100-year-old man. Interesting. Unfortunately, we're sitting on a stockpile of millennium human-interest pieces and I'm afraid we're running out of time to show them all. And a story coming from San Diego is not quite as local as I would prefer. Plus, after January 1, these kinds of stories will have little appeal.*
>    *There's still an outside chance we might run it, but I think that's doubtful under the circumstances. Please feel free to look for other avenues.*
>
>    *Keep in touch,*
>    *Bob*

Shelly was stunned, her entire body feeling sick. Sitting on a stockpile of millennium stories? What kind of bull was that? Her film was so much deeper.

She hated rejection.

* * * *

Once again, John was carefully searching through boxes, drifting in and out of memories, hoping to find a hint of perfection with a trace of order. As always, he found much of it moving and relevant. He knew it was good, damn it. And that was the problem; that it still just sat there, only for him to read, nobody else, a total waste.

He came across some songs he had written before he had met Jessica, when he still had a wild idea of someday being a songwriter or even a performer. He tried to recall the melodies. By modern standards, he supposed, these were probably outdated. Then again, there was also the distinct possibility he had been so far ahead of his time that his stuff might still be viewed today as cutting edge.

> *The last thought that she had as her lover left her bed,*
> *"I cannot live without something new."*
> *His eyes tried desperately to return to the routine,*
> *"Under all my weight, can't you move, love?"*

John uncovered a song he had called *Forgotten Dream*, noticing he had circled the last two lines.

> *The sun was gone when the clouds burned away*
> *It happened so fast I could not move.*

He found an entire pile of songs.

> *I stood on the shore and refused to yell*
> *Somehow content to hear the ocean's roar.*

*Bash Down the Walls*? He could not even remember that one. But here was a song he did recall, written in 1930, *I Would Like to Live on the Prairie*. The song was about an old man, of all things.

As he read the words, it struck him hard that as a young man he had somehow grasped the essence of old age.

*All the old man needed was someone to love*
*Someone to hold him as a child*
*Someone to soothe him with their gentle hands*
*Somehow to keep away the storm.*

He had recalled taking a different direction at the end of that song, the music from his piano becoming both simple and haunting.

*Life is a lost and a wondrous rage*
*I don't want to be afraid to be alone.*

And somehow, as he slowly hummed the song, he could not help but think about Shelly.

\* \* \* \*

John assumed it was a dream, but wasn't quite sure. Because, really, the room seemed to be as it always had been, at least for a moment. Yet, it was not the surroundings that interested him.

She was beautiful. Although he was certain he had never seen her before, it was odd that her eyes would lock into his, that her smile would be so relaxed and friendly.

And why was she touching his arm?

"John," said Shelly, "is something wrong?"

He turned away, looking for something in the room that might be ordinary; a clue as to where he was, who he was.

"John," he heard that name again. Perhaps this woman was

mistaking him for someone else. His name was not John. His name was . . .

What was his name? It would certainly come to him . . .

He once again noticed the stranger's beautiful face. She seemed to look at him with great concern.

She moved closer, putting both of her arms around him and drawing him gently to her body. He didn't understand what was happening, but he felt safe and warm.

"John," she said quietly, "it's okay."

Who the hell is John?

\* \* \* \*

Shelly couldn't get it out of her mind. Bob Beatty should have loved her video. Despite what he told her, she knew there was always room for a good story. Maybe he hadn't even watched it. He was probably rushed, his mind elsewhere.

Even so, she didn't have the clout, or the nerve, to ask him to reconsider. Perhaps she'd send an email just to thank him for considering her work and asking if there was anything technically wrong or if he had any suggestions. No, that wouldn't be wise. If she pushed too hard, the guy would never hire her for anything.

Then again, the video was exactly what he had wanted. She'd watched thousands of TV news stories and this was as good as anything else these stations ran. She knew quality and this was outstanding.

It was probably exactly like he had said—no time, no space and this fell outside the L.A. news area. What she should do is try to sell it to a San Diego station. But with only two days left until the New Year, why force it? Considering the millennium overkill, who would even notice a work of art? And three minutes on the evening news wasn't even close to the original intention of the film. Had she forgotten this was supposed to be a full-scale documentary? Something with depth and meaning, something that might win critical acclaim and a few important film awards, something that would vault her into fame. Just because the TV thing didn't work was no reason to quit. She assured herself that it would be better to wait.

Or was she simply procrastinating?

Goodness, she thought, I'm turning into John Hammond.

# CHAPTER 17

Friday, December 31, 1999. How strange.

John was taking an unhurried and hopefully comforting morning walk. Temperatures were supposed to reach the mid-sixties by afternoon, but the Southern California sun already felt warm. He took slow, deep breaths.

It would not be official until 11:59 p.m., but John had evidently managed to reach his goal. One hundred years ago today, he thought, trying to recall what it was like when the world was young. As he did on every birthday, this would be the proper moment to put his life into perspective, weigh the victories against defeats, dreams that had disappeared, avenues he chose foolishly to ignore. So much he would do differently if offered the impossible chance.

John could hear his mother's voice.

"You boys keep an eye on Sarah," she said.

Hadn't she just ordered them to move away from her? Scolded them for playing baseball too close to their little sister? At their mother's insistence, they had deliberately moved their game of catch.

"You can't even throw straight," John had yelled at his brother.

"I throw better than you," countered David. "You just can't catch."

"You gotta look where you throw," said John. "How can you ever be any good if you don't watch what you're doing?"

The ball bounced twice in the dirt and skidded past him. John chased after it, grumbling that David had no arm or brain whatsoever.

"No wonder you like the Pirates," bellowed John. "None of them can throw either."

"You're crazy," chattered David. "Are you saying Honus Wagner can't throw?"

John noticed that Sarah was walking toward the woodpile. She knew she was not allowed to be over there. He would stop her.

"Pittsburgh's much better than the stupid Giants," continued David.

That was simply not true.

"The Giants can beat the Pirates any day," yelled John as he turned to throw the ball back to David, somehow forgetting about Sarah, as if an argument about baseball was more important than the life of his little sister.

He had noticed her heading for trouble. He had meant to grab her, to pull her back where it was safe. It would have been so easy.

John had never told anyone that he had seen Sarah heading for her death. He never mentioned that he decided to chase a baseball rather than save his sister's life.

John stopped his walk to rest his hand on a fence, catch his balance, regain his breath; but he could not relax his mind, he could not shake that one moment, that one piece of wood that forever changed the world.

He was positive his mother's death was caused by the devastation of losing her youngest child. She had no chance.

And what about David? He turned cynical, brutal, his bitter

writings continually badgering finality to reveal its ugly face. He invited death into his life as if it were company on a weekend visit.

Mary became haunted, seldom venturing outside her own creativity, certain that death was a bandit awaiting the slightest advantage. And so it would be.

If only John would have realized what he was seeing when Sarah walked toward the woodpile. If only he had altered his path for just a few stupid seconds. He might as well have picked up the log himself, dropped it on Sarah's head and spent the last 90 years in prison.

It was strange that no one had ever blamed him.

Father, however, must have known that his daughter's death was John's fault, that someday he would find vengeance, and quietly waited until he could forever destroy what his oldest son loved the most.

Was that possible? Had it been revenge?

During the times his mind would descend into that unbearable cavity, John had always supposed the old man was sick and frightened; that George Hammond had somehow thought his granddaughter would make his own death easier, that their souls would live forever, together.

No matter his father's reasoning, it might never have happened had John rearranged a few stray moments of his life back in the summer of 1910 to ignore his brother and protect his sister.

And, of course, John's wife would not have died. Jessica would have seen their daughter grow. They would have had more children and grandchildren, but for that one moment.

John, his mind rapidly clicking, suddenly realized he was walking much faster than his body could handle. Slow down, breathe.

But now he could see the cliff, feel his baby falling silently through air without cushion, a straight 538-foot drop to an unsympathetic earth, dirt punctuated by rock. And the authorities would speak of impossible odds, velocity, crushed bones.

What must it have been like for his dear lost girl?

No doubt she had total trust in her grandfather. Still, did Sarah sense the old man's insanity or just drop to her death without knowing? Certainly, she was too young to comprehend the delicate balance of life, to process fear. Just a tickle in the stomach as she fell, a drop of rain splitting against the naked rock, a crash so absolute that pain was never registered, death never realized.

"Sarah's been dead for half a century," he muttered to himself, "and probably still doesn't know it, or have the slightest notion she was ever alive."

"Stop," John commanded, putting his hand to his eyes, trying to cry, to scream, to block evaporated tears that had long been drained.

And John could now see Jessica tracing their daughter's journey; finding the precise spot on the cliff's unstable ledge, focusing her anguished mind on the exact point of impact.

What thoughts could have been exploding within her ravaged mind? Was the plunge but an instant or did it turn to slow motion as she carefully processed the inventory of her life?

The flash of birth, a parent's warmth, childhood friends, a first kiss, her love for John, Sarah's smile . . .

And, once again, he saw Jessica falling; her arms surely reaching out for her baby, her eyes searching for a secret passageway, her tortured existence grasping for a miracle.

John realized there was never anything he could have done to change his wife's intentions. For Jessica, it was an easy decision. She loved their child more than she needed him. There would be more comfort in death than life.

\* \* \* \*

John stopped, puzzled by the surrounding houses and fences and lack of trees. Where was he?

Don't panic, he thought, just turn around. He couldn't be lost. But, still, there was nothing familiar about this place. He should backtrack a little way and hope to see a house or street where he had been before.

It worked.

He knew this neighborhood, exactly where he was. There was no need to worry. He had only been confused for a moment.

It would be best to return home.

\* \* \* \*

John stopped when he reached the yard, closed his eyes and put his face toward the sun. And the fullness of its warmth brought back one more memory. Nothing special, just an instant of his life.

Jessica was standing over the crib, singing a lullaby. Sarah was maybe six months old, nearly asleep to the soothing sounds of her mother.

And John watched them both, certain that he was the most fortunate man in the universe, that he had everything he could ever desire right here in this room.

And there was one other thought housed in the back of John's mind from that night so far away as he watched his beautiful wife sing to their baby. He distinctly remembered thinking that this one beautiful moment would last forever.

# CHAPTER 18

It was less than three hours before midnight, the year 2000, when John finally woke from a deep sleep. There had been noise, but he was too tired to stir. He also had experienced another vivid dream, but he could not remember any details, just traces, then nothing.

It struck him that because he was born in the east, three hours ahead of California, he was already 100 years old. What the hell . . .

An hour later, he was showered and dressed to party. Originally, this was supposed to be a small gathering. But now the house was crowded with colleagues, relatives and friends of Daniel and Katherine. Some of them looked familiar, but John could not recall any names. A few wished him a happy birthday and New Year. Most of them kept their distance or didn't seem to notice him at all. He couldn't avoid feeling a bit awkward, beginning to wonder if he might be happier alone in his room.

Still, he was not about to miss this event and slowly roamed through the crowded house, searching for the comfort of a calm conversation.

Someone was saying it had been at least 50 generations since the last time anyone celebrated a new millennium. Another person was predicting this would probably be the final millennium since the world would undoubtedly have blown itself

221

to bits well before the next 1,000 years rolled around. A man in his thirties was commenting that the 20th century had a certain warmth and safety, that it was almost sad to say good-bye.

John gazed around the room, feeling a strong twinge of jealousy. Mostly, these people could care less about conclusion. They were celebrating a beginning.

"Can you imagine what the world will be like 100 years from now?" Daniel was saying to one of his friends. "Technology will have snowballed so fast that absolutely anything will be possible. We might even be able to live forever. Wouldn't that be a kick?"

"I'll be happy just to make it to dawn," Daniel's friend inserted, both of them laughing.

John felt a hand press lightly on his shoulder. He turned slowly, his eyes instantly struck by her beauty, the main organs of his body in various stages of detonation.

"Hello stranger," said Shelly. "You look like the most interesting man at this party. Mind if I hang out with you?"

John was taken back. She was kidding, wasn't she?

"I don't think I've ever seen a more beautiful woman," he said, staying with the mood she had set.

"Thank you," she said. "And you are certainly handsome."

He needed something to come back with, but couldn't figure what to say. Too late, she changed direction.

"I'm not going to start filming until just before midnight," she said.

"I liked it better when I was calling you beautiful and you were telling me I was handsome," said John, surprised by his boldness.

"You're smooth," countered Shelly. "I bet you say that to all your lady friends."

Actually, he'd been looking for a line like that for about 85 years.

"Only when I honestly mean it," he said.

Shelly moved closer, put her arms ever so softly around him, her warmth and smell skyrocketing his body and mind.

"Happy birthday, John," she said quietly.

* * * *

The night moved much faster than John had envisioned. For some reason, he had pictured time actually slowing down out of respect for this momentous event. As Shelly was hoisting her camera, Daniel grabbed a small microphone he had rented and quieted the crowd for a special announcement.

"Ten minutes until the new millennium," he said as everyone applauded, "but we have another extremely important occasion to celebrate before then. At 11:59 p.m., exactly 100 years ago, my good friend, John Hammond, was born. And, if you do your math, you'll realize that by midnight, John will have lived in three different centuries."

The crowd seemed to gasp.

"Way to go, John," someone quipped.

A few others laughed and applauded.

Then Daniel led them all in singing *Happy Birthday*. It was silly, embarrassing, bizarre, and sort of fun.

"John," Daniel blurted into the microphone, "how about a few words?"

Daniel should have warned him. The last thing John needed was to talk about himself to a bunch of strangers. But suddenly the microphone was in his hand, the crowd looking his way, the camera moving close.

Too late now, he thought.

"I was born in the Susquehanna Valley of Pennsylvania," John said, "where it hit midnight about three hours ago. Hey, I'm already 100."

Laughter.

Of course, this was an easy crowd to humor; most of them were juiced.

"I've lived a good life," John said, "and known many wonderful people. I wish they all were here tonight."

This is a stupid speech, John was thinking, but noticed that several of the people were crying. Daniel, however, was looking at his watch, seemingly eager for John to wrap it up.

"When I was a kid," continued John, "I made a vow that I would live to be 100 years old. Despite the odds, I've somehow managed to pull it off, to win the big game. So, where's my prize?"

Applause, laughter, tears. Daniel reclaimed the microphone as several people came up to hug John or pat him on the back.

"One minute to midnight," roared Daniel as if he were Dick Clark.

And the countdown began, ending in an explosion of streamers, screams, laughter, and kisses. Outside, fireworks pelted the night sky. All over the world, people were singing, making love and killing each other. The new millennium had struck.

The energy John had felt several minutes earlier had disappeared. He was 100 years old, had touched three centuries, he was tired.

And the people around him celebrated.

\* \* \* \*

It was late, the house near empty, lights turned low and the mood quite soft. Daniel and Katherine were slowly dancing to an old tune by the Platters.

> *My prayer*
> *Is to linger with you*
> *At the end of the day*
> *In a dream that's divine*

Perhaps it was the mood of the music, but Daniel kissed his wife with a tenderness reserved for young lovers.

Shelly had put away the camera equipment and was now by John's side. She put her hand on his back and slowly rubbed. John could feel his strength returning. God, he loved this woman.

"This is a perfect night," he heard her whisper. "I'll be your prize."

\* \* \* \*

Shelly came to him that night.

Once again, the pit of his stomach was feeling hollow, anxious. The muscles twitched, the throat turned dry. Surely, he thought, the ancient stains of his body would be lost in the darkness.

"I love you so much," she whispered.

He tried to speak, but couldn't.

She tore away her clothes, the light from a candle revealing a smooth and firm body, even more beautiful than he had so often imagined. He removed his shirt, his heart racing faster. She was so tender, so exciting. And he felt young, strong, alive; as if this love broke all barriers of time.

They touched again, their naked bodies sweltering with passion and emotion and joy. Locked into this one moment of perfection, his strength was ignited. He simply could not tell where his body ended and her body began.

It was crazy, it was magic, it was all he had ever wanted.

Slowly, suddenly, from within her warmth, he noticed a gentle and overpowering white light. At first, it had been at a distance, but it was rapidly gaining in strength and intensity, now totally encompassing his being.

He gently pulled himself away from Shelly. It would only be for a moment and he would certainly return to her, but the bright light was so fascinating, so wonderful, so perfect.

And he was calm, totally relaxed, like a child in his mother's arms.

\*\*\*\*

Then both the light and darkness vanished.

# CHAPTER 19

In July 2045, when Shelly Kingston bought the rights to *The Brave Historian*, her friends in the film business called it a huge risk. Sure, it had been a bestseller with multiple printings, but that had been years ago. In fact, *The Brave Historian* had been the first of nine John Hammond novels, all published after his death. The list also included: *The Man with Total Control, 1945, Pirates Ships, The Last Living Child of India* and *Go Down West Virginia*.

Published in 2016, Daniel Stroud's *The Unfinished Works of John Hammond* had been another bestseller. Stroud also had added personal remembrances about the man many considered the most gifted novelist of the 20th century; mentioned in the same breath with Hemingway, Faulkner, Steinbeck, Wharton, Camus, Kafka.

Stroud's initial break occurred in 2001 with the release of Shelly Kingston's award-winning documentary film *Three Centuries on Earth: The Life of John Hammond*. It was, of course, Kingston's big break as well, her steppingstone into motion pictures.

Armed with the contents of two dozen cardboard boxes, Stroud hooked up with a publisher and, within six months, had quit his teaching position to work full-time editing the volumes of John Hammond's writings, beginning with *The*

*Brave Historian.* With all of the Hammond novels to his editing credit, plus the anthology of John's unfinished writings, Daniel was putting together *The Scattered Thoughts of John Hammond* when he and his wife died in an automobile accident during the summer of 2019.

At the Academy Awards ceremony in the spring of 2050, *The Brave Historian* won five Oscars, including Best Picture. The Oscar for Best Director went to Shelly Kingston, the fourth time in her illustrious career that she had been so honored by the Academy.

Accepting the award, Kingston thanked only the living, those people who had meant so much to her career and those who might still influence it.

And it struck her several days later that she had made a terrible omission during her acceptance speech. Even if John Hammond was long dead, Shelly should have thanked him most of all. If anything, he had taught her to focus and push her creativity. Without realizing it, he had fueled her realization that you can never stop short of your goal.

One of the last things John told her that New Year's Eve half a century ago was that reaching 100 was hardly an achievement; that he could have been so much more.

"I was always afraid to take a chance," he had said.

That was just a couple hours after midnight, Shelly recalled. The guests had all gone home. Shelly and John were sitting, quietly talking. Daniel and Katherine Stroud were dancing to a slow and beautiful love song; she couldn't remember the name.

Shelly remembered putting her hand on John's fragile back, that he had mumbled something about love and beauty, had called her name, then closed his eyes and died.

She had greatly admired the old man, but after half a century, his memory had become lost to the past.

# THE BRAVE HISTORIAN

\* \* \* \*

Shelly was 78 years old now; a powerful and wealthy celebrity with a long list of successful films to her credit. With good health and modern vitamins, her career might still have another 20 years. She still had ideas and goals.

Fame, creativity and faith had resulted in a comfortable life. The other corners of Shelly Kingston's existence, however, had become a quagmire. She had been through three marriages, but nothing even close to the love she had envisioned as a child. Nor did she have children, an irrevocable choice she often regretted. Shelly was certainly not looking to marry again, although it wasn't that her chances weren't ripe. Even at her age, she was quite attractive and did seem to meet plenty of apparently interested men. But she had learned to be cautious. Besides, she was always busy working.

She had friends, success and wealth. But there was no family left and she often felt lonely.

Late at night and deep into sleep, she sometimes dreamed of a lover with dark and sensitive eyes. He would come to her with truth and passion, hold her tight, yet let her breathe.

She knew they were just silly thoughts of sentiment and fantasy. But it was his eyes she always remembered.

"I love you," he would whisper. And she knew he wanted to say more, but somehow couldn't.

It was always understood, in her dream, that she loved this man just as deeply, as if their souls touched at the very thread of the universe and time had no boundaries.

And it was strange, because she could vividly remember every moment of these dreams, as if they were real.

# THE END

# About the Author
## ROBERT D. GAINES

Born into a naval family in 1945, Robert (Bob) Gaines was raised in California, Rhode Island, and Virginia. Even as a child, he had an obsession for recording his stray thoughts into hundreds of notebooks.

After graduating from San Diego State University, Bob would spend a decade as an award-winning sports columnist before moving east, eventually retiring from Bucknell University in 2012.

*The Brave Historian* is the fifth book he has published. Other works include: *The Three Mathewsons* (Hidden Shelf 2012); *The Christian Gentleman: How Christy Mathewson's Faith and Fastball Forever Changed Baseball* (Roman & Littlefield 2015); *Loose Chronicles: Dog from a Distant Universe* (Hidden Shelf 2017); and *One Christmas Lasts Forever* (Hidden Shelf 2018).

Bob currently resides in the beautiful mountain town of McCall, Idaho where he spends his days writing, hiking, and playing with an energetic goldendoodle, Rocky.